MW00962024

FLOORS II

Three Below

Patrick Carman

© 2021 by Patrick Carman

No part of this publication may be produced in whole or in part, or stored in a retrieval system, or transmitted in any form or by any means, electronic, mechanical, photocopying, recording, or otherwise, without the written permission of the publisher.

All rights reserved

PC Studio, Inc.

Four blocks over and twenty-one blocks down from the Whippet Hotel, there was a crumbling neighborhood of mostly empty buildings. Somewhere in that neighborhood, at the end of its darkest alley, a man stood before a grim door. He'd walked down six concrete steps to arrive at the door, where he stood, unsure of what he should do next. His elbow had caught the edge of a spiderweb on his way down, and he nervously brushed it away.

Twice already he had raised his hand to knock, only to pull it back and consider his options. He could return to his basement cubicle at the New York tax office, where the ceilings were lit with awful yellow buzzing lights and his cell phone wouldn't work. All day long he stared into a computer screen looking for mistakes on forms. It was a thankless, depressing job, for which he was paid only enough to afford a one-room apartment in the very neighborhood where the grim door stood.

His name was Mr. Carp, and he hated his day job. It ran the risk of turning him bitter like the burnt coffee they served in the basement.

Any casual observer would see how Mr. Carp's whole awful existence appeared to well up inside him — his mangy cat, Claudius; his threadbare couch; a total lack of interesting hobbies; basic cable.

He was a man, it seemed, with nothing much to lose. And so, against his better judgment, he knocked on the forbidding door.

He instantly turned to leave, as if he knew it was a mistake. When his foot touched the last concrete stair and he was about to make his escape into the dismal gloom of the alley, the door opened.

"Mr. Carp, what a pleasant surprise."

It was a sharp voice, filled with the kind of power that stopped sad, desperate men in their tracks. Carp looked back and tried to be polite.

"Ms. Sparks, I presume?"

"The one and only," she answered, tapping the edge of the door with her long fingernails. She eyed the attaché case under Mr. Carp's arm and smiled wickedly. "Come in, then, come in. I've just put on the tea. We'll have a nice long chat, us two."

Ms. Sparks leaned out the door as Mr. Carp came back and stood beneath the shadow of her large beehive hairdo.

"I have some business to discuss," Mr. Carp said, anxiously straightening his wire-rimmed glasses as he stared up into Ms. Sparks's narrow eyes. He had a thick, tangled-looking mustache, which he ran his hand over nervously.

Although Ms. Sparks did not seem impressed, that was all part of her act. She knew this was a visitor of some importance, for Mr. Carp had the power to turn the fate of the Whippet Hotel in a different direction.

The grim door shut and a secret conversation was had.

· CHAPTER 1 ·

A WEDDING AT THE WHIPPET

There is no better place on earth for a wedding than the roof of the Whippet Hotel. At least that's what Leo Fillmore thought as he watched six yellow ducklings waddle down the grassy path toward him. They had rings of delicate white flowers from Mr. Phipps's garden tied around their necks. Now and then, the ducklings would turn clumsily with the idea of eating the flowers, but looming overhead they saw Betty, their mother, staring down at them. Any ideas about eating flowers before they reached the pond quickly vanished.

A mariachi band strummed three guitars in perfect unison as a robot the size of a coffee cup arrived at the top of the grass pathway.

"Here comes Blop," Leo's best friend in the whole world, Remi, said, straightening his tie nervously. "I hope he can stay quiet long enough to get down here." Remi had a round face and brown skin like his mother.

"Stop worrying," Leo said, patting Remi on the back. "Blop knows better. He's got this."

"I wouldn't be so sure," Remi said, and he might have been right to worry. Blop was a terrible chatterbox.

Both Leo and Remi were anxious as Blop weaved back and forth toward them with bubbles rising out of his metal belly button. As the bubbles climbed into the air, they popped, freeing glitter that fell like sparkling snowflakes over the gathering of people.

"Nifty trick." Remi smiled. "I was afraid he was going to burp the ABCs."

Blop whirled all the way down to the edge of the pond and aimed his head like a cannon over the water.

"Time for his big finale," said Remi. "I hope it doesn't backfire."

A circle opened on Blop's round head and there was the sound of swooshing air as small daisy petals shot up and showered down over the pond.

"Amazing how many of those will fit inside such a small space," Remi observed, but mostly he was glad the whole thing had gone off without a hitch as Blop zigzagged back to where the boys stood.

Leo smiled and gazed over the pond, where the ducklings were chasing one another around glowing lanterns floating on the water. When the petals started to land all around them, they were at once confused and elated. They were too young to realize that petals did not normally fall from the sky, so they simply did what ducks do: They gladly gobbled up whatever fell their way.

Leo, too, looked up into the night sky, thinking how strange it was that at age eleven he owned this remarkable hotel. It was a lot of responsibility, but he'd done a fine job keeping it running during his first year on the job. All around him were tall buildings full of light, encircling the Whippet Hotel like centurions. He searched for Merganzer D. Whippet, the man who had built and formerly owned the hotel, wondering if he would appear.

Meanwhile, Blop whirled to a stop next to Remi. "That was harder than it looked," said the robot, staring up at the two boys as the last of the bubbles drifted up and away. And then, "Not much of a view from way down here. Just a lot of shoes and —"

"Shhhh," Remi scolded, picking up Blop and placing him gently into his jacket pocket. When Remi looked up again, Leo's dad was coming down the path. Clarence Fillmore might be the head maintenance man at the

Whippet Hotel, but tonight he looked like a movie star at the Academy Awards.

"Mr. Fillmore cleans up better than I expected," said Mr. Phipps, the gardener, leaning down and whispering to the boys.

"He'll be back in his overalls by morning, you can bet on it," Leo joked, but he had to admit, his dad did look like a million bucks: clean shaven, hair in perfect order, dapper in a tuxedo and shiny black shoes. He arrived next to the boys, smiled at them both, and took up his position next to a remarkable sculpted green bush, one of Mr. Phipps's masterpieces: two green doves standing three feet high, filled with dots of light, and between them, a silver plate holding two rings.

"You've outdone yourself, Mr. Phipps," Clarence Fillmore whispered.

But the Whippet gardener (and, on this night, its justice of the peace) ignored the compliment. His attention was riveted elsewhere, and as Clarence Fillmore followed the gardener's gaze, he understood why.

It would be said for years after by everyone in attendance that Mr. Fillmore and the doves and the floating lanterns, the bubbles and ducklings and flower petals, the quiet buildings towering overhead on every side and all the rest — it *all* paled in comparison to the person who arrived alone at the top of the grassy path just then.

There came a hush over the proceedings. The guitars stopped playing and even the ducklings stopped swimming on the slick surface of the water.

The bride had arrived on the scene.

"Wow," Blop said from Remi's pocket, but that was all he could manage. Even for the most talkative robot Mr. Whippet had ever constructed, Remi's mom was unexplainably beautiful.

Mr. Phipps finally cleared his throat in the direction of the band and they stirred awake. "Here Comes the Bride" played on three guitars as she began to walk. Leo felt his dad trembling beside him.

"Steady, big guy," he whispered. "You're going to make it."

Pilar smiled nervously as she came down the path. The train of her dress was long and white, and her smile was contagious.

When she arrived next to Leo's dad, she unexpectedly leaned down to Leo's level and looked into his eyes.

"We have something for you, will that be all right?"

She had a Mexican accent — soft around the edges — that had always enchanted Leo, so it was possible Pilar could have said "I need to kick you as hard as I can right now, will that be all right?" and Leo would have nodded just the same. Pilar glanced up at Mr. Fillmore for one last sign of assurance, and he nodded knowingly. The two of them had talked about what was about to happen, and they had agreed it was the right thing to do.

And so it was that when Pilar stood, she also waved gently in the direction of a gathering of bushes next to the small pond. Out of the darkness came Captain Rickenbacker and Theodore Bump, two of the Whippet's long-stay tenants. Captain Rickenbacker lived on the third floor in the Pinball Machine and had long imagined he was a superhero. On this night, he wore a black cape in the style of Batman, and in his hands he held a box covered with an equally black velvet cloth. Theodore Bump had been at the hotel forever and a day. He wrote novels by the dozen and kept mostly to himself, but tonight he was staying close, making sure Captain Rickenbacker didn't drop whatever it was he was carrying.

"I don't remember this from the rehearsal," Remi said, but his mother looked at him in a way Remi knew all too well: *Be patient, you will see.*

Captain Rickenbacker walked with an important sort of stride, and when he reached the two carved doves, he set the box on top of the silver tray. Then he stood aside and Mr. Bump removed the black velvet cloth so Leo could see what was underneath.

"It's a full moon," Leo's dad said. "We planned it this way."

A glass box sat on the silver tray, and inside, a white ghost orchid was quiet and sleeping. It had been his mother's special flower, the one so hard to grow.

"The moon will wake her up," said Pilar.

Leo looked at Pilar, who was about to become his new mom. It was very hard to think about replacing his real mother, but she'd already been gone such a long time. There were days when it was hard for Leo to remember what she looked like without taking out her picture. The silver tray was at Leo's eye level, and as he stepped toward it, the ghost orchid began to bloom in the soft moonlight on the roof of the Whippet Hotel.

"So you know she is always here with us," Pilar said. "With our family. Is this okay?"

Leo wiped a tear that had found its way to his cheek. He couldn't take his eyes off the orchid, so peaceful and perfect, just like his mom had been.

"It's okay," Leo said, and it was. Pilar was going to be his mom, and it was going to be fine. He smiled wistfully at her and his dad, then looked at the flower once more as it reached out toward them all.

The wedding vows were said and the band roared into gear. There was a lot of dancing and laughing and cake-eating. After a time, Mr. Phipps took the glass box to the safety of his garden shed, because like a special memory, a ghost orchid is a fragile thing.

When the dancing really got cooking, Leo let Ms. Pompadore return to her room and get Hiney, her yappy little dog. Ms. Pompadore had been paying her way as the concierge since Leo had taken over the hotel. As a former Texas socialite, the task fit her like a glove. If a guest needed tickets to a show or information about a museum, Ms. Pompadore was always there with a snappy answer.

"Just keep Hiney away from the ducks," Leo said. "You know how they get with each other."

"I'll carry my little Hiney, not to worry!" Ms. Pompadore was gone in a flash, leaving Remi and Leo to giggle.

Now and then a very important person doesn't show up for a wedding, the kind of person who is missed but not mentioned because it makes everyone a little sad to remember they are at a party without that special you-know-who. *Maybe he's only trying to make a surprise entrance and he will show up after all,* everyone thinks. Such was the case at the Whippet Hotel wedding as a one-of-a-kind blimp secretly drifted between two sky-scrapers, its full shape coming into view directly behind the pond. No one noticed it at first, because the pilot of the blimp was being crafty about his business. And the blimp was special in the way it reflected light, so that it was very hard to see if a person wasn't looking for it. But then, suddenly, the blimp lit up with a message, written out in bright lights along its curved side:

CONGRATULATIONS, PILAR AND CLARENCE!

Everyone on the roof looked up and gasped.

"I had a feeling he might show up unexpectedly." Captain Rickenbacker smiled.

"I have a great urge to return to my room and write this all down," said Theodore Bump, but instead he whipped a pen out from behind his ear and began taking notes on a wedding napkin.

Everyone was enchanted, beguiled, overwhelmed with happiness as Merganzer Whippet leaned his head out over the crowd and bowed, a great top hat falling, falling, falling off his head until it landed in Pilar's outstretched hand.

"Oh dear," said Merganzer, touching the wild flop of hair on top of his head. "I've dropped my hat."

"Come closer!" yelled Pilar, laughing along with everyone else. "I'll throw it back to you!"

But he vanished once more inside the cab, blasting a shot of hot air into the blimp to hold it steady. Mr.

Powell, Merganzer's oldest and dearest friend, emerged for a split second and waved, yelling hello. And then he, too, was gone.

"The blimp is passing over," said Pilar. She was a sad bride, which is one of the saddest things in all the world. "I wish he could stay."

"Wish granted!" Merganzer shouted, throwing a long rope ladder down one side of the cab. Mr. Powell did the same from the other side, and soon the ropes were secured and two figures were climbing down to join the party. Betty waited at the bottom of Merganzer's rope ladder, honking excitedly.

"Oh my, you've gone and had ducklings again," said Merganzer, kneeling down to Betty and putting his long hand out toward her. The ducklings gathered around and nudged against his legs, for they knew a lover of ducks when they saw one. Merganzer laughed, pointing his tremendously long nose up into the air, and the music, which had stopped, began playing again.

"May I?" Merganzer asked, looking at Clarence Fillmore for permission to dance with his new wife.

"By all means, dance all night if you want!"

Pilar tried to return his hat but he told her to keep it, so she put it gamely on her own head and began teaching Merganzer how to cha-cha.

Mr. Powell was not a dancer, so he stood with Leo and Remi near the gift table.

"Where have you been all this time?" Leo asked, because the two of them hadn't been seen in almost a year.

"Near enough to know we weren't needed," said Mr. Powell. "You're doing a fine job with the hotel, a fine job indeed. If there's one thing Merganzer knows how to do, it's get out of the way when he's no longer needed."

"Isn't it enough that we miss him?" Remi asked. He took Blop out of his pocket and set him on the gift table, where the robot could whirl around and examine the packages.

"I'm afraid being missed isn't enough," said Mr. Powell. "He's very busy. Many important things to do."

"Busy doing what?" Leo asked. "And where?"

Mr. Powell looked at Leo as if he'd gone mad.

"Making things in the field of wacky inventions, of course! What else would he be doing?"

This was an exciting idea for Leo, and he thought seriously about scaling the rope ladder while no one was watching so that he could stow away to the field of wacky inventions and see what was going on there.

"What sorts of things is he making?" asked Remi, gazing up at Mr. Powell with big, round eyes.

"Secret things."

"But those are the best kind!" complained Remi. "And besides, we can keep a secret. Can't we, Leo? Tell us just one thing he's working on, won't you?"

Leo wasn't going to beg. If Remi wanted to, that was fine. But Leo would sooner dance the cha-cha than grovel for information. George Powell asked about the finances and the guests and the state of things at the hotel, but he would say no more about wacky inventions.

When the dance ended, Merganzer hugged Pilar and walked around the roof, taking a moment to talk to each and every guest. The blimp seemed to be pulling harder in the wind as Merganzer tapped a special key card and blasted more hot air inside to hold it steady. Everyone gasped with delight when the blimp lit up. They all wished he would stay, but it was becoming clear he would be leaving them again, and soon.

Leo and Remi left Mr. Powell with Blop and joined Merganzer at the rope ladders.

"Can I look inside?" asked Remi. The cab was way up in the air and Remi was short and round, so seeing inside would take some effort. Merganzer studied the boy carefully.

"I think maybe not," he said. "There are complicated controls in there. This is no ordinary blimp."

"How so?" asked Leo. He pretended as if he only cared a little.

"Can't say, too perilous," Merganzer replied. Leo loved the way Merganzer always made everything sound *dangerous*.

"You have to go again, don't you?" Leo asked. He was feeling sorry for himself as he thought about all the fun he and Merganzer had shared in the past.

"I'm afraid so," said Merganzer, crouching down beside Leo and Remi. "Very important work to do, can't wait. Tonight will have to be enough for now."

"For now?" asked Leo, a rise in his voice at the idea that maybe a day was coming when they might be together on an adventure again.

Merganzer only smiled, but the smile was enough to cheer the hearts of the two boys. It told them all they needed to know: Someday they would spend entire days with Merganzer D. Whippet.

"I may have a need or two," said Merganzer, standing up and staring down at Leo and Remi. "Rather soon, in fact."

"We're ready now!" said Remi.

"I do like your enthusiasm. Await my instructions; it won't be long now."

Mr. Powell was already climbing up one of the rope ladders, like he was late for an important meeting.

He was unexpectedly swift for an older man with a potbelly.

"Come along, Merganzer," he yelled down from the cab. "The wind has shifted to our advantage. It's time to go."

Merganzer took one last look around, tapped Betty on the head, and raced up the ladder with alarming speed and efficiency. Just before he reached the top, he turned once more to the crowd.

"It's the loveliest wedding I've ever seen. You've done the Whippet proud."

"Merganzer, we really must be off," said Powell, reaching down toward his companion of so many years.

When Merganzer D. Whippet was in the cab, the rope ladders were released and the blimp began to rise. Against all matters of science and nature, it moved against the wind, but it didn't surprise Leo or Remi one bit.

"He can go wherever he pleases in that thing," said Leo. "He's not fooling me."

"Me neither," said Remi, folding his arms across his chest. He paused a moment, glancing at Leo out of the corner of his eye. "When do you think he'll need us?"

Leo shrugged. He had no idea. *Soon* could mean hours, days, years. One never knew with Merganzer D. Whippet.

Merganzer leaned out of the cab as it sailed away and yelled one more thing to Pilar.

"Look inside the hat!"

He waved and was gone, the blimp passing behind a building and up into the night sky on its way to secret places only Merganzer and Mr. Powell knew.

"Maybe it's taped to the inside," Leo heard his dad say. They were having trouble finding a gift inside the top hat.

"I think you're right!" Pilar said, reaching her arm way down inside (it was a very tall hat) and taking hold of a black envelope. When she pulled, the hat collapsed in on itself, flattening out like a pancake.

"Weird hat," Captain Rickenbacker said, standing at the ready just in case it was part of an evil plot designed to strip him of his superpowers.

Leo divided his attention between the stacks on the gift table and the people gathered around the hat shouting, "What is it? What is it?" The gift table was long, and Blop was at one end along the edge, rolling around as Leo picked up different boxes and shook them.

"It's a letter," Leo heard Pilar say, which got his attention. Merganzer's letters always led to something interesting. Looking up at Clarence, Pilar held out the black envelope. Merganzer D. Whippet had wild handwriting that could be difficult to read, but Clarence

Fillmore knew it well. He'd been reading Merganzer's maintenance notes for years.

While Clarence opened the letter and everyone waited breathlessly for what was inside, Blop discovered something unexpected on the gift table.

"This one isn't for the bride and groom," he said. The robot had come across a brown, leathery-looking envelope with a red wax seal. "It has your name on it," Blop told Leo, but Leo wasn't listening. "And Remi's, too."

Blop talked so much that most people chose to tune him out. He was like background noise in a coffee shop. Which was why Leo hadn't heard about the brown leathery envelope with the red wax seal. He was, instead, listening to his dad as he read the letter from Merganzer D. Whippet.

"'Go to the south side of the roof and look down. Your carriage awaits.'"

Every single wedding guest ran to the south side of the building and leaned out, searching the grounds for whatever the letter might be referring to. Leo couldn't be sure, but it almost felt like the top of the hotel bent down toward the ground as everyone crushed to one side. Was that even possible? He was reminded once more of the many ways the Whippet Hotel could surprise him.

"Sir, did you hear what I said?" Blop had rolled back down the long gift table and was now staring up at Leo, trying to get his attention, but Clarence had arrived at the side of the building with everyone else as they caught their breath and pleaded with him to keep reading. Below, at the entrance to the Whippet Hotel, were two large horses and a carriage sparkling with thousands of white lights.

"Um . . . okay . . ." Clarence said, looking again at the letter. He'd already read it to himself and, taking Pilar's hand, he read it out loud so everyone could hear.

"'It's time Pilar showed you her part of the world in style. A seven-day cruise through the Mexican Riviera should do it. All the plans are in order, everything is paid for. Leave the kids behind, as they'll be busy running the hotel in your absence. You're flight leaves tonight! Away to your packing!'"

Remi had arrived alongside Leo, and the two of them glanced at each other with a mischievous grin. No parents for a whole week and the entire hotel to explore? It was exactly what they both wanted to hear.

"No one's staying in the Flying Farm Room," Remi whispered.

"And Captain Rickenbacker will totally let us play pinball," Leo whispered back.

Blop kept on talking about the envelope, but there was a lot of commotion drowning him out. Besides, Leo and Remi were too busy thinking about all the fun they were going to have as soon as their parents left the country.

It took some convincing to get Pilar on board. She desperately wanted to go, but it was so extravagant, and she'd never left Remi alone for an entire week. But Remi insisted it was no big deal, he'd be fine, and the bridesmaids were practically bursting with excitement. Soon they were all hurrying down to the carriage for a closer look, leaving Remi and Leo to plot their plans in peace on the roof.

"Is there any chance either of you might listen to me, because if there's not, I'd like to get back in Remi's pocket and take a nap," Blop complained.

"What's that you say?" asked Leo, finally looking down at the chattering little robot.

"I said there's a gift on this table that's not for the bride or the groom. It's for you and Remi."

"Really?" Remi said, taking a keen interest. "Maybe it's candy or comic books."

Leo told Blop to lead the way, and the two boys followed until they came to the envelope.

"Are you thinking what I'm thinking?" Leo asked Remi.

"I sure am," said Remi.

Leo picked up the envelope and gently broke the wax seal.

"Mr. Powell must have left it here," said Remi. "He's sneaky."

Leo popped the wax seal off the envelope and pulled out two things. One was a letter, the other a key card.

"Whoa," said Remi, taking the card and turning it in the soft light. "That's the coolest hotel key card I've ever seen."

And it was. The card was black, but then it wasn't. As Remi turned it in the light, the color changed from deep green to burnt orange and everything in between. When he held the card still, it went black once more.

"Is there liquid inside that makes it do that?" Leo asked no one in particular.

"I'd have to take it apart and examine the insides to find out," Blop said. "Let me have a closer look."

But Remi knew better. If Blop got ahold of the key card, he'd waste no time trying to break it open and experiment with it. He had tiny arms and claws that were surprisingly good at destroying things.

"It's from Merganzer," said Leo, and his heart leapt. Maybe it wouldn't be a quiet summer at the Whippet after all.

"Hang on! Don't read a word without me," Remi said, running to the six-tiered wedding cake and loading up two glass plates. He returned and the boys sat on the grass.

"Okay, here goes," Leo said, taking a big bite of cake and then talking with his mouth full. The penmanship was even worse than normal, and Leo guessed that it was written from the blimp as it flew through the night sky, bumping along on gusts of wind.

> Dear Leo and Remi,
>
> I have a slight problem that will require a small favor, and I know you two are perfect for the job. My apologies for needing to get rid of your parents for a while, but it simply had to be done. They would never have let you go because the slight problem and the small favor are terribly dangerous. Parents can be so very ... safe. It will be much easier if they're not around.

"This is starting to sound awesome." Remi smiled and shoved a huge chunk of wedding cake into his mouth.

> The slight problem is embarrassing. I neglected to mention the state property taxes for the hotel. (Ms. Sparks always took care of such things, and it

slipped my mind.) If memory serves, you owe about $700,000 for last year.

"Uh-oh," said Leo. "This is starting to sound not so awesome."

"Keep reading!" Remi begged.

"Okay, okay," Leo said, and went on

The key card will help you solve this little problem. And you'll be able to do me that small favor. I need some things from the hotel subbasement. Important things. You'll find them on the way, and some people, too. They will help you. I wish I could say more, but really, I shouldn't. If you knew where this adventure was going, you wouldn't do it. I've said too much!

"He has a weird way of asking for favors," Remi commented.

And yet, it was somehow the perfect invitation. It would be dangerous, so much so that if they knew *how* dangerous they wouldn't go at all.

It was exactly what Leo and Remi needed to hear.

"There's a subbasement in the Whippet Hotel?" Leo couldn't believe it was possible, an entire basement he knew nothing about.

There was one more part at the end of the letter:

Ask Betty, she'll know what to do with the key card.
Off with you now! Time is of the essence!

Your friend,
Merganzer D. Whippet

It was bad enough they were expected to pay a year's worth of back taxes Leo hadn't planned for, but getting important information from a duck in order to use the key card? It was ridiculous.

"Where are we supposed to get seven hundred thousand dollars?" asked Remi. He pulled out his nearly flat wallet and counted out the crumpled bills. "I have four bucks."

"I bet there's plenty of money hidden in this place," Leo said. "I just can't believe there's a basement we didn't know about. I thought we knew this place inside and out."

In truth, Leo and Remi were about to discover just how little they really knew.

CHAPTER 2

FOUR FLOOGERS, A ZIP ROPE, AND THE IRON BOX!

Mr. Carp scratched his scruffy mustache nervously as he fidgeted in his chair. If Ms. Sparks had been able to grow a mustache, she would surely have grown it very long, with handlebars for twirling between her bony fingers. Sitting in her dank apartment across from a low-level, weasel-faced tax agent was making her day. Misery, it seemed, really did love company.

"I don't know how you do it, Mr. Carp. It must be murder in that office, shuffling papers all day, and no air-conditioning. It's deplorable."

"They treat us like swine," said Mr. Carp. He was glugging iced tea by the glass and eating the stale cookies Ms. Sparks had set on the table as if he hadn't eaten since breakfast the day before. Ms. Sparks took notice of the black grime under Mr. Carp's fingernails and thought he must be a mechanic of some sort in his off time. And a bachelor for sure, without someone to tell him to wash his hands.

"So we have a deal then, am I right?" asked Ms. Sparks. It was all she could do not to jump up and down with excitement, but she had to play it cool. She couldn't scare him off.

"It's very sensitive information, you understand," he said. He'd already mentioned this fact eight or nine times, and it was starting to grate on Ms. Spark's nerves. Her fingernails tapped on the table but she kept her wits about her, the prize in sight.

"Of course it's sensitive, I completely understand. But you do want to get out of that basement, don't you, Mr. Carp? And I can make that happen. I know just the person we'll bring this offer to. He's perfect."

"But are you sure you can trust him? I mean, it's Merganz —"

"Don't say that name!" Ms. Sparks boomed. She'd managed to lose her cool after all. "I can't stand that pointy-nosed ingrate!"

Mr. Carp dropped the cookie he'd only just picked up.

"I'm only saying," he said, reaching delicately for one more cookie. Ms. Spark's evil eye bore down on his hand, and he pulled it back. "Well, it's just, he's very popular in the governor's office."

"Of course he's popular!" Ms. Sparks yelled. She could blow a person's hair back with her voice. It was that big. But she calmed herself, brought her voice down, and continued. "Merganzer D. Whippet is lining the pockets of all those bureaucrats. He takes care of *them*. But what has Whippet ever done for *you* besides leave you to rot in a basement? And *me*? HA! He never appreciated me, never gave me a dime I didn't work double for. He's worth billions! Trillions! Zillions! Don't you want a piece of that, Mr. Carp? Don't you *deserve* it?"

Mr. Carp wanted to point out that Ms. Sparks had used Merganzer's name a couple of times and he hadn't been allowed to, but her eyes were bulging out of their sockets far enough that he thought they might shoot right out of her head. He didn't like being bossed around, never had. But at least this time it might get him somewhere.

He reached his hand out over the stale cookies and snatched up one more.

"We have a deal," he said.

Ms. Sparks stared at Mr. Carp with a deep look of cold satisfaction. She would be the boss of this deal. He would do as she said. And if things worked out in the end, he'd get his reward.

"Time for me to make a call," she said, picking up the thick manila envelope Mr. Carp had brought with him.

Mr. Carp glugged the last of his tea, snatched up two more cookies, and went for the door.

"Be ready to move," Ms. Sparks demanded, leaning forward toward him as she stood holding the door. "This is going to happen fast."

Mr. Carp nodded and moved out from under the shadow of the beehive hairdo. When he was on the other side of the door, he proceeded up the steps in the manner of a possum: low and nervous, like a truck might barrel through the alley at any moment and squash him flat.

Before Leo and Remi could escape into the labyrinth of hidden Whippet Hotel tunnels, Mr. Phipps returned to the roof and ushered them both downstairs so they could say good-bye to their parents. It was a celebration and all — the carriage and the laughing and the well-wishing — but it took longer than either boy was happy about. They endured a prolonged debate between Pilar and Clarence Fillmore over whether they should stay or go. One minute they were in the carriage, the next they were mercilessly hugging the boys, overcome with guilt about leaving them behind. They were family now, and families stuck together.

It was nice to be fussed about, but really, all Leo and Remi wanted to do was get rid of their parents for a week so they could go exploring in the hotel. The hotel was in a lull, with hardly any guests at all, so they could run free if only their parents would get out of the way. As the clock struck ten, they knew the secrets of the strange key card would have to wait until morning. If there's one thing Leo wouldn't do at the Whippet, it was bother Betty after ten. She was always grouchy at that hour and preferred biting over helping.

Eventually the carriage pulled away with Pilar and Clarence Fillmore inside.

The hotel grew quiet and peaceful.

"This seems like a bad omen," Remi said. Both boys had slept fitfully and woken early, leaving Blop to recharge for a few hours. Standing on the front steps of the hotel, eating leftover wedding cake and squinting into the morning sun, they watched as a black limousine rolled through the front gate.

"Are we expecting someone?" Leo wondered out loud. He'd looked at the guest book and seen that it was, as was often the case, blank for the day. There were the long-stay tenants, but they knew how to navigate the weird world of the Whippet just like Leo and Remi did. And their checks never bounced, which was saying something, given the outrageous price of a stay at the hotel.

"There's only one family I can think of that would show up without a booking and start throwing money around," Remi said.

"The Yanceys," Leo said, stuffing the last of the cake in his mouth and wiping his hands through his thick, curly hair.

"That's gross," Remi complained. Remi was a big eater, but he was also a little bit of a neat freak.

Jane Yancey popped out of the car holding a cherry Popsicle, which was dripping down the side of her arm.

"I'm going up!" she yelled, throwing the Popsicle into the grass and racing for the front steps. No doubt she had been dreaming of the Cake Room all morning and couldn't wait to get her hands into some frosting.

"Hello, *Jane*," Remi said. He was not a fan of spoiled, demanding seven-year-olds, and Jane was a pro at both.

"Out of my way, stupid!" she said, barreling by Leo and Remi like she owned the place, and giving Remi a sharp elbow to the gut for good measure on her way past. Leo turned and nodded at Ms. Pompadore, who was running the front desk in Pilar's absence.

"Let's see how long they're staying," Leo said. "Play it cool, bro."

Remi nodded as Nancy Yancey, Jane's mother, glided out of the car in a red silk dress that looked like it might have cost more than the limo. He made a mental note not to allow Captain Rickenbacker near Mrs. Yancey, at least for today. The Captain was known to shoot paintballs at large moving red things.

The driver had been carefully unloading suitcases and he was already on the seventh one. "How long will you be staying?" Leo asked Mrs. Yancey, starting to worry the Yanceys might remain aboard for the summer.

"No greeting? No cold drink?" asked Mrs. Yancey. "Your standards are getting lower every time we visit. I'll have to tell Hubby about that."

Mr. Yancey appeared from inside the car dressed entirely in black, phone at his ear. He was still very bald, the sun gleaming off his head like everything above his eyebrows had been covered by a plastic sandwich bag. It was altogether possible that he was never off the phone.

"If I had a kid like Jane Yancey, I'd stay on the phone all day, too," Remi whispered. "I bet there's no one on the other end of that call."

"You might be right," Leo whispered back. So many bags! Twelve or more. The poor driver was sweating like a boxer in the tenth round, and the bags were winning.

"You'll need to bring those up to the room," said Mrs. Yancey, breezing past Leo and Remi into the cool of the hotel. It was unclear who she was talking to — the driver or the boys — but the driver wasn't taking any chances. The Yanceys were clear of his car, and he knew them well enough to know he wasn't going to get a tip.

"Bill my office," Mr. Yancey said out of the side of his mouth, then he was back into the conversation he was having about layoffs in the Denver office. The limo sped away, leaving a pile of bags in its dust.

Leo was starting to wonder whether or not he could leave the running of the hotel to LillyAnn Pompadore and Mr. Phipps. What if something went wrong? Only Leo knew how to fix a broken pipe or an air-conditioning unit.

Mr. Yancey finished his call and looked at the hotel.

"I loathe the Whippet," he said, without any concern over what Leo might think. Then he took in the whole of the property the Whippet sat on. It was enormous — an entire corner of a city block, and most of it was empty unless you included the pond, the grass, and the towering bushes carved into the shapes of animals. He looked at the property as if he wanted to own it, which was not surprising. Every zillionaire in New York wanted to own the land the Whippet sat on.

"Has she arrived yet?" asked Mr. Yancey. He'd been lost in a daze and didn't realize what he'd asked until it was too late.

"Who, sir?" asked Leo.

"Yeah," Remi added. "Who?"

Mr. Yancey looked at the pile of bags and then back at the two boys.

"Never mind. Just get the bags upstairs. I'll wait outside and make a few calls. Better hurry. You don't want to upset Nancy Yancey on a travel day."

Leo and Remi each grabbed two heavy bags and carried them up the wide stairs to the double doors.

"Let's get these bags delivered and find Betty," said Leo. "I have a feeling something isn't right. The sooner we figure out how to use that new key card, the better."

As Mr. Yancey looked all around the property in every direction with an evil grin on his face, it was clear that Leo was right to worry. The only time Mr. Yancey smiled was when he was looking at something he might soon add to his empire.

The Whippet had always been exclusive and mysterious. It was never really meant to operate like a normal hotel with the burden of real guests. People like Theodore Bump and Captain Rickenbacker were fine. They took care of themselves, more or less. They understood the way of things at the Whippet. But once in a great while someone did have the money — like the Yanceys — and the unexpected interest — the Yanceys again — and the Whippet had to operate like an actual hotel.

"I tried to get rid of them, but Mrs. Yancey didn't even flinch when I said the price per night had doubled," Ms. Pompadore told Leo.

"At least we'll make some money," said Remi. "We could use it."

"How long are they staying?" asked Leo.

"She wouldn't say. And you know Mr. Yancey — he's always on his phone. He just handed me a gold credit card and walked away."

"Keep an eye on them, will you?" asked Leo. "Remi and I have something we need to do. It might take a while."

"Yeah, like a week," Remi murmured under his breath.

LillyAnn Pompadore took this as a joke and waved them away. She was fully capable of taking care of the hotel . . . as long as nothing big went wrong.

Finding Betty was easy, because it was a summer morning and all the ducks were swimming in the pond on the roof. It took some bread crumbs to lure her out of the water, and all six of the ducklings came along. They stared up at Remi when the crumbs were gone, and Remi dug into his red bellboy jacket pocket for more.

"I'm running a little low here," he said. "I didn't expect seven mouths to feed. Show her the card, quick." Remi dropped another handful of crumbs and the ducklings fought over them as Betty looked on.

Leo whistled softly, holding the card out for Betty to see. When she noticed it, she honked loudly in Leo's face.

"It's working!" Leo said. Obviously Betty had seen the card before, because she was actually standing on Leo's feet, trying to get a better look. "You know this card?" he asked, holding it a little bit closer as it changed colors in the sunlight. He held it too close, and Betty half flew, half jumped into the air and chomped down on the card. She got the card and Leo's thumb, and Leo yelled, pulling his hand away.

Just that fast, Betty was now in possession of the key card Leo and Remi had been given, a card that was supposed to lead them to seven hundred thousand dollars and a dangerous adventure.

"Perfect," said Remi. "She's going to eat the key card!"

Betty couldn't quack without letting go of the card, so she made an awful wheezing sound instead, like she'd swallowed a giant marble and couldn't cough it up.

"This is bad," said Remi. "First the Yanceys, now this."

Leo shook the sting out of his thumb and moved in low, trying to coax the key card out of Betty's mouth. The ducklings stared up at Remi, quaking excitedly for more crumbs. When Betty turned slightly to one side, Leo leapt toward her head, reached out, and grabbed for the card. Ducks are faster than they look, and the pond was closer than it seemed, so Leo missed the duck and landed facedown in the water. His maintenance overalls, with their many pockets and tools for carrying and fixing, were soaked.

"Come on!" Remi yelled. "She's getting away!"

Betty was waddling quickly away from the water, but the ducklings were only interested in more bread crumbs. They were nipping at Remi's pant legs, so he took the last of the bread crumbs and threw them into the pond. They passed Leo coming the other way and darted off in different directions before landing in the pond, swimming for crumbs.

"Run!" Leo said, passing Remi and grabbing him by his coat. "She's heading for the duck elevator!"

Sure enough, that was exactly where Betty was going. It was a small elevator, barely big enough for two boys and a duck, and by the time Leo and Remi caught up to her, Betty was standing inside, staring at them both.

"We've got her cornered," said Remi. He looked at Leo, then back at the duck. "She bites hard, huh?"

They both wondered if getting into a tiny space with Betty was a good idea or not. It might be the same as sitting in a car with a badger, something that would involve a lot of biting and screaming. Leo inched closer, talking softy to Betty, until his body blocked the door.

"They're coming back," said Remi, hearing the ducklings getting out of the water. "They eat like little horses!"

But Leo wasn't listening. Betty had set the strange key card on the floor of the duck elevator and was pushing it toward him with her bill.

"Come on," Leo said. "Let's get in."

"Wait, what? Are you crazy?" Remi complained. "She'll duck-bill us to death."

Leo crouched low and sat inside with Betty, staring at the card but not picking it up.

"There's not going to be room in here for both of us and seven ducks," Leo said. "Get in here!"

Remi looked at the ducklings. They were eager for more food and, actually, they weren't that small anymore. They were growing up fast. If they got him on the ground, Remi imagined, the six of them could really do some damage.

"Move over," he said, squeezing in next to Leo. Betty stared at them both, then at the ducklings, then honked in Leo's face. Her breath smelled like pond water.

"I think she wants you to shut the door," Remi said. He was intuitive with animals that way, always had been. "She wants a break."

And it was true. The ducklings weren't as young as they'd once been. They were demanding, and Betty did like the idea of getting away for an hour, a day, maybe even a week.

"It's not like they won't get fed," Leo said, thinking it through. There were mechanical feeders on the roof that filled with orange pellets twice a day. The ducklings would be fine.

"Let's do it," said Remi.

As soon as Remi closed the door, he pulled the down lever and the duck elevator began its leisurely descent to the lobby of the hotel. It was a magnificently slow elevator.

Betty turned away from both boys, staring into a corner, and for a moment Leo thought she was either sad or angry. He was dangerously close to the back end of a duck in a very small space. It was terrifying.

"How much do you trust this duck?" Remi asked.

"Not that much," Leo answered. "She can be unpredictable."

Leo carefully picked up the key card and turned it in his hands. He'd fallen asleep the night before doing the same thing, trying to find a clue to its secrets. It was dimly lit in the duck elevator, but he saw the same patterns of color in the card. Blues and purples, reds and greens, appearing in a line down the long end of the card, kind of like the bar on the back of a credit card, the one you swipe through a machine to pay for groceries.

"What's she doing?" Remi asked, peering like a mind reader around Betty's feathery rear end, up her long neck, and into the very thoughts of the duck itself. She was staring at the corner of the duck elevator, as if there should be something there. She was completely still, focused.

"Let me see that card," Remi said, and Leo handed it to him. They were only halfway to the lobby and Leo was already getting tired of the thick smell of wet duck.

"I see what Betty is staring at," Remi went on, gently reaching over Betty's head and placing the edge of the card into the top corner of the elevator. It had seemed like a normal corner, but it was not. There was a thin gap there, about double the length of the long edge of the card. Without thinking twice, Remi inserted the card and swiped downward slowly. As he did, the elevator walls changed — they danced with color! — and Betty quacked and hopped up and down excitedly. When Remi pulled the card out, Betty backed up, crowding the boys into corners of their own. She was hogging the very center, staring down. The walls of the elevator returned to the milk-chocolaty color they had been. For a few seconds, nothing else happened. But then the soft sound of the elevator moving came to an end.

They had stopped.

This, in and of itself, was not that unusual. Leo had stopped the elevator many times and gotten out into secret passageways that ran between the floors. The same door they'd entered would open, and out he would go. But this time it was different, because a different place opened than had ever opened before. Or at least Leo had never seen it happen.

A wall simply dropped down, like it was on rollers that let it slide below the elevator. This was unfortunate for Remi, because he was leaning against it. Remi was a little bit on the round side, and before Leo could get over the fact that a wall of the duck elevator was no longer there, Remi was falling backward through the opening.

Leo was a lighter boy by almost half, but he grabbed Remi by the ankles, hoping he could somehow hold on. Remi's tube socks rolled down in Leo's hands until his fingers reached the shoes and the shoes popped off like two bottle caps.

"Oh no!" Leo yelled. For a split second he thought he'd gained a brother only to lose him one day later in a horrible elevator accident. But then Betty jumped through the opening, too, and Leo heard the sound of a duck bill chomping on something crunchy. Maybe the duck elevator was closer to the bottom of the hotel than Leo had thought. He peered slowly over the edge and found Remi and Betty four or five feet below. Both of them were eating.

It's a known fact that Whippet Hotel ducks love animal crackers more than any other treat. And Remi liked them, too. They'd landed in what appeared to be a separate shaft, next to the duck elevator and filled with animal crackers. Remi dug deep and threw handfuls up into the air. The crackers rained down on Betty, who caught one on the drop and swallowed it whole.

"I thought I was a goner there for a second," said Remi, popping a crunchy, monkey-shaped cracker into his mouth. "Best cookies *ever*."

"No wonder Betty wanted to come in here." Leo smiled. "She must have known about the card and the cookies."

"C'mon down, there's something you should see." Remi's words were garbled because his mouth was so full.

Leo wasn't so sure about leaving the safety of the elevator. What if it left without them? How long could they live on animal crackers with no milk to wash them down?

Instead, Leo hung his head into the open space, the blob of curly hair on his head nearly reaching the pile of cookies below. He saw what Remi saw, only upside down.

There were two slots in the bottom of the elevator, like the ones on a hotel door where a key card could be inserted to unlock the door. To the right of each slot was a symbol. The symbols were these:

- *A tree*
- *A glass beaker*

"What's this do?" Remi asked, reaching toward something that was on the wall.

"No, don't!" Leo said. He was worried the button Remi was reaching toward might send the elevator wall back up and cut him right in two, like a magic trick gone terribly wrong. But Leo was too late to stop Remi and his insatiable curiosity.

Leo closed his eyes, waiting for the wall to slam into his chest, but instead he heard a familiar voice.

Merganzer D. Whippet was back.

"Don't let Betty eat too much or she'll throw up in the duck elevator. And I hope you brought gloves. If you haven't . . . actually, never mind. It will be fine."

It was Merganzer's voice, but he wasn't there. The voice had the scratchy sound of a recording, and Merganzer was acting distracted, like he was doing nine things at once and his mind was only partly on the task of leaving a message. There was a pause in which Merganzer yelled something out of range, probably to Mr. Powell.

Leo dropped his arms over the edge and craned his neck so he could look at Remi. He pointed to one of his hands. *What did he mean about the gloves?* Leo said with his eyes and his hands, but Remi just shrugged, picked up a handful of animal crackers, and set them in Leo's outstretched hand. Betty stole one with her lightning-fast bill. She was eating a lot.

"*Can't talk long, much to do!*" Merganzer's voice was back. He was always busy, but Merganzer D. Whippet was never specific about anything he was doing, only that it was all very important and there was never enough time.

"*If you're not Leo and Remi, then you've gotten extremely lost in the hotel. Push the green lever down. And never get in a tiny elevator again.*"

Merganzer started banging on something Leo and Remi couldn't see. It sounded like he was hammering dents out of a car door, waiting patiently for someone to leave in case the card had fallen into the wrong hands. Remi was slowly reaching for a green lever, but Leo slapped his hand away just in time.

"Are you nuts? The floor probably falls out and sends you, Betty, and ten thousand animal crackers down a twisting slide going a million miles an hour!"

Remi liked the sound of that and began reaching for the green lever again.

"Not funny," Leo said, but he couldn't help smiling. Remi was the most curious kid in the world. He was the best.

Merganzer's voice resumed. *"Now listen carefully, both of you. No more dilly-dally, no more fiddle-fuddle. All business! The card will work for the first subbasement — the one with the tree. The other key you'll have to get along the way. Visit the floors in order; it's the only way. You'll find the money and some other items I'm in desperate need of. You must bring these items back to me! Ask for them by name: four Floogers, a zip rope, and the iron box. Can you remember? You WILL remember! Say it once more."*

Remi was like a zombie on cue: "Two flumpers, a burp bag, and the ironing board."

"Excellent!" said Merganzer's voice.

Leo rolled his eyes as he tried to reach out and grab Betty but missed. She was really eating a lot of animal crackers and he wished he could get her back up in the duck elevator so she'd stop.

"Everything will be fine, just fine," Merganzer's voice said, which meant he had no idea how things were going to go. *"You can get more fuses from Dr. Flart — he should have a few of them lying around. And if you're really in a pinch, ask Ingrid — she's got one. Also, Blop has one of the special fuses inside him. Just take off his head."*

"Fuses?" Leo said.

"Who's Flart?" Remi said. "And who's Ingrid? And what's this business about taking Blop's head off?"

Remi reached his hand into a place under the elevator Leo couldn't see while Leo considered the situation. Maybe the duck elevator had blown a fuse he didn't know about. As a second-generation maintenance man, his mechanical brain was spinning with ideas when Remi held out his hand.

"He must mean this."

This time, Remi wasn't holding an animal cracker. Instead he held a glass tube the size of a roll of pennies. It had a series of twisting red and green wires inside and metal caps on each end.

"That's not like any fuse I've ever seen," Leo said. "Better be careful with it."

"There's also this one," said Remi. He pulled something loose and held it up in his other hand. The same fuse, only this one was charred with black soot.

"Blown," Leo said. "And it looks like it's been that way for a while."

Remi started to put the new fuse in place, but Merganzer's voice (and Leo's arm) stopped him.

"Don't put the fuse in until you're sure you're ready to go. It will take you to places you've never been. Dangerous places. But you can do it! I know you can! I trust you."

Remi beamed. He loved being trusted with important things to do.

"Give me the fuse," Leo said, and Remi handed it up. Leo could hang down and insert the card and the fuse when they were ready. It would be a snap — at least until the door flew up and pinned his arms to the ceiling.

Leo dug around in his overalls for a metal fuse grabber, which was a lot like a pair of pliers only it had soft, curved grippers for grabbing delicate objects.

"Remember!" Merganzer boomed once more. *"Four Floogers, a zip rope, and the iron box!"*

"Two flip-flops, a zonker, and a sneeze!"

"It's really not that funny," Leo said. "This is serious."

"Oh, right. Sorry," Remi said, but inside he was giggling. Zonkers and flip-flops and sneezes hit him square in the funny bone.

"One last thing and you're off. Very important. You'll need some instructions for later, but you should get them as soon as you can. You'll find the instructions in a secret place."

There was a slight pause, like Merganzer was trying to decide if he should continue, and then he did and it made no sense at all.

"An isle of Penguins, a boy named Twist, Robinson Crusoe!"

"He's gone completely mad," Remi whispered, but Leo was used to the puzzles and the rants. He and Merganzer went way back.

"You'll have to grab Betty," Leo said, and suddenly he knew why Merganzer had mentioned gloves. "There's no other way."

Betty was turned away from Remi, eating animal crackers as fast as her orange bill could pick them up. Remi hadn't picked up a duck before, but Leo had. He was fairly sure it would not go well.

"You can't just lift her," Leo said, placing the clamped fuse in the front pocket of his overalls. "You'll have to grab hard and throw her up here. Otherwise she'll get loose and bite you."

"Thanks for the warning," Remi said. He filled his red jacket pockets with animal crackers and rubbed his hands together for good luck.

"Here goes nothing," he said, and lunged for Betty. He got his arms around her big middle and hugged, but as Leo had suspected, Betty was no dummy. She bit down hard on Remi's finger, which made Remi raise his arms and throw the duck over his head. Feathers were flying everywhere and Betty was quacking loudly, but she was back in the duck elevator and Leo was up on his knees, blocking her way out.

"Nice job!" Leo yelled. "Throw me some crackers!"

Remi shook the sting out of his finger and started picking up fistfuls, throwing them up into the elevator until Leo told him to stop. This seemed to calm Betty down, and she went to work on the thirty or so treats on the floor while Leo reached down and hoisted Remi up into the space. It was totally cramped inside again, and Betty started acting weird. She sat down, burped, then burped again. The third time she burped was more violent. A slobbery, projectile animal cracker launched from her throat and tagged Remi in the side of the head.

Leo went to work on the fuse, prying it into position as he leaned down over the edge of the opening and hung upside down.

"Incoming!" Remi yelled, shielding himself behind his red jacket. Betty burped again, this time shooting Leo in the butt with a slobbery thing that had recently been a giraffe cookie.

"Hurry up!" Remi said. "She looks like she might go machine-gun mode on us!"

Leo had the fuse in place and it hummed with red and green light.

"Cool," he said, for Leo loved all mechanical things. He slid Merganzer's special key card out of the side pocket of his overalls and inserted it into the top slot. The tree next to the slot glowed green. Pulling the card out, Leo moved as fast as he could back into the duck elevator.

For a moment, nothing happened.

Then Betty burped up an animal cracker, which flew over Leo's head and caught in his hair.

"I'm just glad she eats them whole," Remi said. "This could be a lot worse."

The wall suddenly shot back up with alarming speed. Betty became very still, like she'd seen this happen before. She hiccupped and sat down.

Then something scary happened.

It felt like the cable snapping in two overhead.

The duck elevator was free-falling, and as Leo and Remi and Betty screamed and quacked and burped up animal crackers, the duck elevator zoomed past the lobby, gaining speed.

It kept going, and going, and going . . . far below the Whippet Hotel, to secret places few had ever seen.

· CHAPTER 3 ·

THE JUNGLE ROOM

The duck elevator slowed from out-of-control fast to very slow in the blink of an eye. This made Leo and Remi feel like they were being squashed, pinned to the floor by an almost unbearable gravity. When it stopped completely, they were left dizzy and confused.

How long had they fallen, and how far?

How would they get back up?

And what was that noise from the other side of the door?

"Where are we?" Leo wondered out loud. He hadn't gotten up the nerve to open the small door because of the noise he heard. Something was moving out there.

"I wish we'd brought Blop with us," Remi said. "He'd know what to do."

Betty shook her head and wobbled to her feet. She had a certain look in her eyes Leo knew all too well.

"We need to get this duck out of here," he said.

"Why? I don't think we should," Remi argued. This was becoming a little more adventurous than he'd bargained for.

"She needs to use the bathroom," Leo said. *"Now."*

Whatever was outside couldn't be more frightening than Betty using the duck elevator as a bathroom with Leo and Remi stuck in the same space.

"Ready?" Leo asked.

"Not really," Remi answered, but looking at Betty, he knew they were out of options.

Leo pulled the lever that opened the door, but only enough to see out through a small crack. He peered out, listening, watching. Whatever had been out there was either gone or hiding.

"Cool," Leo said.

"Let me see," Remi said, nudging Leo aside and pushing his face up against the crack in the elevator door.

"Leo?" he said.

"Yeah? It's cool, right?"

"Something just touched my eyeball."

Suddenly the doors flew open and Remi jumped back.

Two boys and a duck stared into the open space, where a monkey the size of a football stood staring at them. It had the brightest green eyes they'd ever seen, so bright they seemed to glow in the soft light.

"Is it just me or is that a really small monkey?" Remi asked.

As he was saying the words, another monkey — same size, same big green eyes — leaned its head upside down from above.

Betty was bigger than either of them and the bravest of anyone inside the elevator. She honked loudly, which sent the two monkeys scattering, and walked away in search of some privacy.

"How many do you think there are?" Leo asked.

Before Remi could answer, the two monkeys were back, and this time they weren't alone. They had brought friends. Lots of them.

"They seem nice enough," Leo said. They weren't like any monkeys Leo had ever seen, and not just because of their size. These monkeys had elf ears, white brows, and dark furry faces that looked permanently startled because of the big eyes. They were covered in black body fur, but all the tails were long and orange, like the extension cords in the Whippet basement.

Thinking of the extension cords reminded Leo that technically he was still in the hotel, but it felt like a different world underground. Remi took out an animal cracker and cracked it into four or five smaller parts, holding his hand out.

"Hey, they like me!" Remi said. The strange little monkeys gathered around and emptied Remi's hand in a flash.

Leo looked past the group of seven or eight monkeys staring at Remi for more food. Out beyond the duck elevator, it was like a jungle under a full moon on a starry night. Vines hung from the canopy of a huge tree that covered the sky. The tree was full of sparkling white lights, like the carriage had been. Back and forth through the branches of the great tree there were rope bridges and ladders. A woman not that much bigger than the monkeys was standing far above on one of the rope bridges.

"Don't feed the Leprechauns!" she yelled. She had a big voice for such a small person, and she was mad. Whoever it was rapidly descended the tree by way of a series of hanging rope ladders, long vines, and rope bridges.

"Leprechauns?" Remi asked Leo. Leo darted out of the elevator just before all the monkeys jumped onto Remi at once. Remi fell on his back and a dozen more monkeys showed up and jumped on top of the first bunch. Orange tails were tangled up everywhere, and the small space was filled with shrieking and grabbing for animal crackers.

"I told him," came a voice startlingly close to Leo. He looked to his left and then down about a foot, and there stood the woman who had been high up in the tree only moments ago.

"You're fast," Leo said.

"Not as fast as the Leprechauns. They're like lightning. Only one way now," she said.

Remi was actually laughing pretty hard, because the thing they later learned about Leprechaun monkeys was that they were completely harmless. They had no claws or teeth, so they could gum you to death, but that was about it. Mostly it just tickled when they clawed, scratched, or bit.

The pint-size woman reached into the duck elevator and started grabbing orange tails. Each time she got ahold of one, she flicked her arm over her head like she was cleaning out a closet. Leprechauns are also incredibly light, Leo soon discovered, because he was asked to help. They weighed about two pounds and didn't have any claws to hold on with, so they really flew when they were tossed.

"Are they going to be okay?" Leo asked.

"Oh sure, they love being tossed around. They live for this stuff," the woman said. She had eyes too big for her head, like the monkeys, and big teeth. They were down to the last four monkeys when she took one by the tail and spun it over her head like a lasso. When she let go, Leo was almost sure he heard the flying creature say "Wooooohooooooo!"

"Those little guys are *hungry*," said Remi, sitting up as the last of the monkeys, who also happened to be the very smallest, burrowed down into the pocket of his red jacket. He saw the small woman and went right to work with the questions. "Who are you? And why aren't you feeding these monkeys?"

The woman, her button nose having turned a little red with the effort, laughed.

"You two must have parents with a million shares of Google stock. I haven't had a guest down here in two years."

"Oh, we're not guests," Leo said. "I own the hotel now. I'm Leo. This is Remi; he's the bellboy."

"And I'm Leo's brother," Remi said, getting up and finally all the way out of the duck elevator. "So technically, I think I'm like an heir to the throne or something like that. What did you say your name was?"

"I didn't," the woman said. She had turned more cautious and curious, like maybe Leo and Remi couldn't be trusted. Betty quacked a couple of times and came out from behind a glob of hanging vines as Leprechauns moved out of her way.

"Betty!" the woman said, softening noticeably. "You're back!"

She turned to the boys, the ice melting off her mood. "I haven't seen this duck in a long time."

She finally said her name was Ingrid and waved Leo and Remi toward the great tree in the center of the underground room. Leo had never seen a tree as big or so full of monkeys; they were everywhere, their glowing green eyes staring down at them.

"If he sent the duck, this must be serious," Ingrid said when they arrived at the wide trunk. "Come on up, tell old Ingrid what's going on. We'll get it figured out."

"Is this really happening?" Leo asked Remi in a half whisper. Remi nodded, and both boys remembered how Merganzer had told them they would meet a person named Ingrid. Remi, for one, was glad that Merganzer had assured them Ingrid could help, but he was *not* excited about climbing the tree. Its roots alone presented a challenge, swarming all over the ground like boa constrictors. He tripped twice just getting to the first rung of the rope ladder.

"How far up are we going?" Remi asked nervously. "Couldn't we just talk down here where it's safe?"

"I think you'll like it better up there. Best view in the whole place."

Ingrid tapped Betty on the head and laughed, then started up the rope ladder like she was related to the monkeys hanging in the trees. She could really move.

An orange tail wrapped around Remi's arm affectionately as he pet the little monkey in his pocket.

"Looks like you found another small friend," Leo said as he put his foot on the first rung.

Remi looked down at the face staring back up at him — incredibly cute, the kind of face that makes you smile and feel better after a hard day.

"Will you catch me if I fall?" Remi asked the Leprechaun. But the monkey didn't understand. It looked up at Remi with those big green eyes and smiled. A monkey loves attention almost as much as it loves animal crackers.

It was some work getting to the top, but mostly it was a blast. Twice they swung on ropes from one side of the tree to the other, landing on vine-covered platforms. At one point the tree limbs became so thick, it was like crawling up through a tangled cave of leaves. When the limbs and leaves opened up again, they found that they'd climbed higher than the tree house by thirty feet. It was nestled against the wide trunk, and it appeared the only way to the front door was by way of a steep zip line.

Ingrid grabbed three zip line rollers out of a wooden box nailed to a limb and gave brief and harrowing instructions on how to proceed. She set the roller over the line, grabbed the two handles, and was gone before either of them could say no.

"Forget it," Remi said, glancing at Leo. "You can't make me."

Six or seven Leprechaun monkeys glided down the zip line by their curled tails, smiling back at Remi and Leo. The tails seemed to rise and fall loosely, like they were made of rubber. Other monkeys followed, riding down the line and jumping off at the bottom. They were a very playful bunch. Leo couldn't help himself — he was dying to fly down to the tree house. It looked like a ton of fun, but the tree house itself was also stirring all the magic places in his imagination. It was SO not what he expected, mostly because it was made entirely of copper and rivets and pipes.

There were three sections to the tree house, different sizes, but all with roofs that looked like the tops of mushrooms, round and curved at the sides. Thick, vine-like pipes ran every which way over and through the three roofs.

"I gotta get down there," Leo said. Looping the roller over the top of the wire, he was gone in a flash. When he reached the tree house, he let go and crash-landed into a clanging metal table. The table sat on a deck of wire grating that ran all the way around the structures. The table hit a metal chair and the chair went skidding off the grating, tumbling down the side of the tree.

"Don't worry about it," Leo heard Ingrid say. "Happens all the time. The Leprechauns will bring it back."

Remi was petrified as he listened to the metal chair bounce all the way to the bottom. He could imagine each and every impact, all the broken bones and, more than likely, a lot of peeing his pants. It would not be pretty.

"Come on, Remi, it's easy!"

It looked for a while like Remi wasn't ever going to make the trip, but the monkeys were nothing if not intuitive, and they liked having company. They wanted to be helpful.

"Loopa!" Ingrid yelled, and the Leprechaun monkey in Remi's pocket popped its head up obediently. "Gather your friends — he's going to need some help."

Loopa was off in a split second, screeching like monkeys do when they're giving orders. Before long, a group of them had taken out another roller and placed it on the line. One of them held it firmly in place while more monkeys than Leo could count started glomming on to the handles. They weaved their small arms and legs around one another, forming a wide loop Remi could sit on.

They all looked at Remi at once and didn't make a sound. They stared so patiently and so forcefully that Remi couldn't stand it.

"You guys have done this before, haven't you?" Remi asked, inching one step closer to the zip line. He should have paid more attention. All at once, dozens of monkeys jumped on Remi's back from the tree limbs behind him.

He didn't have a chance.

The force of many small monkeys landing on him shoved Remi face-first into the loop, and then Remi and about fifty Leprechaun monkeys raced toward the tree house, screaming and screeching. Remi was yelling with fear, but all the monkeys were laughing, or so it seemed to Leo, who was also laughing from where he stood below.

There was a crash at the bottom, like a barrel full of monkeys had blown open, but Remi was fine.

"They'll want to do it again," Ingrid said. "Better get inside and give them a chance to calm down. You've got them riled up good."

She passed through a door, but no monkeys followed, and Leo and Remi went inside. They gathered at an egg-shaped table and got down to business.

"I'm what you might call a gatekeeper," Ingrid said. "No one gets any lower in the Whippet Hotel without going through me. So let's hear it. Why'd Merganzer send you?"

"Can I let her in here?" Remi asked. Loopa was sitting alone at the door, staring in with pleading eyes.

"If I let her in, they'll all think they can follow. Trust me, that's a bad idea. They'll break something. I *never* let a monkey in the house."

"How long have you been down here?" asked Leo. "And how far *down* are we?"

Ingrid laughed. "I thought I was asking the questions! But I can see that's not going to work. You two are either very shrewd or super dumb. I'm withholding judgment."

She stepped across the room on short, stubby legs and opened the lid on a wooden box not unlike the one Leo had seen attached to the tree above. Reaching down inside, she pulled out three glass bottles.

"I get them from Dr. Flart," she said, closing the lid and returning to the table. "He's madly in love with me, but I've got my heart set on someone else."

Ingrid set two of the soda bottles on the table and said something about how a girl wants flowers and dates and more gross stuff Remi and Leo had no interest in. They stole a glance at each other as Ingrid set the top of the third bottle against the edge of the table. She smacked it with the top of her hand and the cap flew off, landing on the floor. There were a lot of caps on the floor, like peanut shells at a ball game, so it was clear she drank a lot of whatever Dr. Flart was sending her.

She held the bottle out to Remi, then opened the other two in the same manner.

"Here's to Remi," she toasted, and they all tapped their bottles together. "For riding the zip line against his better judgment."

There was a commotion outside on the metal grate, where the Leprechauns were putting the chair back in place. Looking into the bottle, Leo got a little nervous. Whatever was in there had started to bubble up orange and frothy.

"Drink up before it starts to disintegrate!" Ingrid shouted. She tipped her bottle back and guzzled all the contents down in six giant swallows. The lady could chug, no doubt.

Ingrid let loose a burp that was so loud and long, both boys were actually a little bit jealous as they stared at their own drinks. The liquid was half gone in both bottles, bubbling and frothing into thin air right before their eyes. Thinking they were already down to half a monster burp, they started gulping.

Seconds later the bottles were empty, and the two boys looked at each other, smiling. They had that feeling of the best burp ever rising up from their guts and, wow, when they let them rip, they were magnificent.

"And it tastes good, too!" Remi laughed.

"Was it grape or lime?" Leo asked.

"No, no — it was root beer and orange soda. No, wait . . ." Remi pondered.

"Let me save you the trouble," Ingrid said. "It's Flart's Fizz, the one and only. Nothing like it in the world."

"You've got to market this stuff! People would go crazy for it! You could make millions," Remi said. He licked the edge of the bottle, but the flavor was all gone.

"Or at least seven hundred thousand," Leo mumbled under his breath.

"Now we're getting somewhere." Ingrid leaned over the table, let out a leftover, unimpressive little burp, and got right to the point. "You two were sent down here for funds, I can tell. He's run out of money again, hasn't he?"

"Not exactly," Leo said, and then he completely spilled the beans about the taxes and owning the hotel, right up to the part about the other things they would need. He didn't get that part out, because Ingrid huffed and interrupted.

"Giving you the hotel is j is just the kind of ridiculous nonsense he's always doing! Is it still standing?"

Remi came to Leo's defense. "Of course it's still standing. Leo is the best second-generation maintenance man in the whole city of New York. And I'm *the* best bellboy."

Remi beamed, but Ingrid just rolled her eyes. She couldn't believe the most secretive, the most important, the most amazing hotel in the world was owned by the kid sitting in front of her.

"Go on," she said wearily. "What else did he tell you?"

"He gave us a list of things to bring back," Leo began. "And a certain amount of money he was hoping to get. Not for us, for the taxes."

"Right, for the taxes." It wasn't clear to Leo and Remi whether she entirely believed them.

"It's, uh . . ." Leo trailed off. "Well, it's seven hundred thousand dollars. That's how much he needs."

Ingrid had one of those stony, hard to read expressions on her face. She betrayed no emotion. Surprise, disgust, relief? Leo and Remi had no idea how to read the immovable object that was her face.

There was a cigar box on the table, and she flipped open the lid, which made Remi recoil in his chair. He'd lived in a building where the superintendent smoked cheap cigars all day long. Whenever the man had showed up at the crummy door to his crummier apartment, he'd blown smoke in Remi's face and laughed as Remi gagged. Remi had grown to despise them. If Ingrid could burp like a sailor, maybe she smoked giant stinky cigars, too.

Ingrid fished around in the box with her hand, searching for something. She took out a brown paper bag and shut the cigar box.

"Did I mention I have asthma?" Remi said, fake coughing for effect. Leo looked at him sideways as Ingrid uncrumpled the top of the bag and pulled out two objects: a pad of paper and a pen. Remi let out an audible sigh of relief and looked back at Loopa, wishing she could come inside. She was hanging from the top of the door by her long tail, swinging back and forth like a ball on a string.

"Take this to the tax man," Ingrid said as Remi turned back around. She had written something on the paper and was ripping it off the pad. Ingrid looked up, smiling, as she began putting things away. "I thought you were going to ask for a lot more. Anything over a million and we'd have to involve the Realm of Gears. You don't want to go down there unless you have to. Very dangerous."

"What's the Realm of Gears?" Remi asked, but Ingrid waved his question away as if it didn't matter, since they weren't going there anyway.

Leo took the piece of paper in his hand. It was official, that much he could tell by the gold leaf edges, the Bank of New York symbol, and the guarantee signed by the sitting president of the Federal Reserve.

"Is that a real signature?"

Remi leaned in close.

"Whoooooooooooa," he said, drawing the word out in a long whisper.

Ingrid pushed her tiny round glasses up on her nose and nodded almost imperceptibly.

"Now," she said, leaning forward on her elbows, "what about that list of things you needed? Let's hear it."

Leo pocketed the note for seven hundred thousand dollars and began to feel a lot better about how this was going.

"I got this," Remi said, putting an arm in front of Leo just as he was about to speak. Leo wasn't so sure after all the joking Remi had done about the list, but he let it pass.

"Merganzer asked us to bring him . . ." Remi stopped for dramatic effect. "He asked us to bring him four Floogers, a zip rope, the iron box, and a bottle of Flart's Fizz."

"Wait, that's not —" Leo tried to say, but Remi elbowed him in the gut. Also, Ingrid had a big reaction to this news. She was up on her feet in the blink of an eye.

"Four Floogers and the iron box?! That's outrageous!"

Remi was pleased she hadn't mentioned the bottle of Flart's Fizz and felt that the small white lie was well worth another world-class burp on the way back to the hotel.

"And the zip rope," Remi said. "Don't forget that."

"Quiet down about the rope," Ingrid said in a half whisper. She motioned toward Loopa, whose eyes had widened into even bigger green saucers.

Ingrid stepped to the door and met Loopa's eyes as the monkey swung back and forth.

"Go and check on the duck; make sure she's not eating the flowers. When you get back you can have a bottle all to yourself."

The monkey was gone almost before the words left Ingrid's mouth. As Ingrid turned to the boys, they could see that her expression had changed. She was no longer only nervous. She was downright worried.

"They live for Flart's Fizz. It's a very, very rare treat."

"Why not give it to them all the time?" asked Remi. He thought the idea of monkey burps was hilarious. If he ran this place, he'd be handing out Flart's Fizz to every monkey in the tree.

Loopa and the other monkeys were gone (they tended to travel in a pack), and Ingrid came back to the table. She was concerned as she looked at the two boys.

"I can't believe he would send two kids down here for the iron box. *And* four Floogers. Very unusual."

"And a bottle of —" Remi started to say, but this time Leo elbowed Remi in the arm and Remi stopped short.

"Why is it such a big deal, Ingrid?" Leo asked.

She walked past them to the box on the floor, kicking open the lid with her foot.

"You can only get Floogers from Dr. Flart," she said. "He's not as easy to deal with as I am. Mad scientists are by nature . . . *unpredictable.*"

Ingrid took out two bottles of Flart's Fizz and set them on the table.

"It's a dungeon down there," she warned.

Remi had been thinking of meeting Dr. Flart and getting all sorts of great stuff he could have fun with. And there were the two bottles of Fizz on the table, which he very much wanted to grab and run away with.

But the way Ingrid said *dungeon* spooked him. He felt a chill in his bones.

"And the iron box," she said, shaking her head. "It's held in a perilous place. One only goes there when one must."

The whole undertaking was starting to sound diabolical to Leo. His responsibility was the Whippet Hotel, and he already had the money he needed to pay the taxes.

"Let's take the payment back to the hotel," Leo said. "Maybe that's all we really need right now."

"I wouldn't count on it," Ingrid said. "Merganzer never asks for something he doesn't desperately need."

Loopa had returned, and this time she sat patiently in the doorway. More monkeys were gathered outside, staring into the tree house from the open windows.

"Don't get too close," Ingrid said. "This will be terribly loud."

Remi and Leo had no idea what Ingrid was talking about as she picked up one of the two bottles of Flart's Fizz and carried it to the door. She cracked it open on the window sill with a loud *pop!* and the metal cap flew into the air. All the monkeys leaned even closer to watch the orange bubbles, their eyes growing larger and greener.

Ingrid got down on one knee and held the bottle out to Loopa. When she did, the very small monkey grabbed it, tipping it into her mouth with lightning speed. All the other monkeys stood transfixed as the contents of the bottle slowly vanished.

Ingrid ran back into the tree house, hiding behind the table like someone was about to launch a water balloon attack.

"Why are you hiding behind the table?" Leo asked.

"Hiding? Who's hiding? I'm not hiding."

Leo and Remi turned in their seats and faced the door, where Loopa's little stomach had stretched to the size of a basketball. It happened fast, too fast for Leo and Remi to react — an earsplitting, high-pitched rumble as Loopa's mouth opened and the burp to end all burps escaped into the tree house. It was a wet, Fizz-flavored burp that blew Remi's hair back and pierced his eardrums. The sound ripping through the tree house was, Leo thought, like the taste of Flart's Fizz: He couldn't put his finger on exactly *what* the sound was. In the same way that Flart's Fizz tasted like all the best flavors rolled into one, the sound of Loopa's burp held many sounds at once, all of them earsplitting and high-pitched. Loopa's cheeks flapped wildly as the burp just kept getting louder and longer until finally, like a balloon emptied of air, she flopped down on her butt with a big grin on her face.

"Is it over?" Remi asked. He'd been covering his eyes and, peeking out from behind a finger, he couldn't be sure if there was another round heading his way or not.

"Yup, that's about it," Ingrid said. "She'll want a nap."

Leo felt a light film of wetness on his face and arms. "Eww," he said, but it smelled pretty good as it evaporated, like Flart's Fizz.

"The thing I don't understand is why he needs so many Floogers," said Ingrid as she walked toward the monkeys, shaking her head with confusion. "That's a lot of power."

"Power?" Leo questioned. "What kind of power?"

Ingrid stood in front of the door and wouldn't look back at the boys. "I've said too much," she whispered, but Leo and Remi had both heard her. They looked at each other, shrugged their shoulders, and tried to imagine what a Flooger was and what kind of power it would deliver. Remi figured that if it was anything like Loopa's burp, a Flooger could probably power a small city for a month.

Ingrid leaned against the frame of the door like she was waiting for something to happen. She looked at her watch and nodded, then Loopa hiccupped and her eyes went very wide. After that, the little monkey stumbled to the edge of the door and curled into a ball, where she appeared to fall asleep.

"One zip rope," Ingrid said, bending down and picking up Loopa's long, orange tail, which was no longer attached to Loopa.

"Okay, that's just wrong," said Remi. "Loopa's tail fell off!"

"Take it easy — she's trying to sleep," Ingrid said softly. She returned to the table carrying the zip rope, also known as Loopa's tail.

"Is she okay?" Leo asked. He'd heard about lizards that could shed their tails if they were frightened by a loud noise or an intruder. But a monkey losing its tail?

"Well, sure, she's okay." Ingrid laughed. "Takes about a month, but it'll grow back. They do love Flart's Fizz. Drives them crazy with delight."

"Is it, you know, *gross*?" asked Remi. He was imagining that only moments ago the tail had been attached to a monkey. Ingrid whipped the tail around like it was a rubber hose. Then she tied the end of it to one of the table legs and started walking out of the tree house. When the zip rope was ten or eleven feet long and still hadn't snapped or oozed something gross, Remi started getting interested.

"That's a super cool monkey tail you've got there," he said.

Ingrid started walking toward them, and the zip rope got shorter and shorter until she untied it and held it over her palm. At rest, it was about four feet long.

"You won't believe how far it will stretch or how strong it is. No one does."

"Ten feet?" Leo asked.

"Twenty!" Remi guessed.

"You two are small thinkers," Ingrid said, smiling as she held out the zip rope.

"More?" Leo asked.

"That's impossible!" Remi screamed, slapping his forehead with amazement.

"Most things in Merganzer D. Whippet's world *are* impossible. I would have thought you'd come to expect that by now."

She got very serious then, opened up the cigar box once more, and took out a key card. It was copper and scuffed, old with use. There was an etching of a science beaker on one side with bubbles coming out of the top. It looked like a key card designed for entrance into a mad scientist's lab.

"Now both of you need to listen to me, and listen good. Merganzer is up to something big. Bigger than the hotel. Even bigger than what's *under* the hotel. Travel carefully. And use this only if you really, really need those Floogers."

"And the iron box," Remi added.

"Yes," Ingrid said slowly, quietly. "And the iron box, too. You'll probably need this."

Ingrid went back to the cigar box one last time and took out one of the fuses required to run the duck elevator underground.

"It's the only one I have, so be careful with it. Without that fuse, there's no getting to Dr. Flart."

Leo remembered Merganzer's words: *You can get more fuses from Dr. Flart — he should have a few of them lying around.*

"One more question," Leo said, putting the zip rope and the scratched-up copper key in the front pocket of his maintenance overalls. He was already thinking of all the ways he could use the zip rope, like jumping off the roof of the hotel, but those things would have to wait. "How many floors are down here?"

"Including mine, three," Ingrid said. "Three below, and more danger the lower you go."

Leo looked at the sleeping monkey, felt the note for seven hundred thousand dollars in his front pocket, and smiled.

He was bound and determined to visit every single floor in the Whippet Hotel.

CHAPTER 4

TROUBLE BREWING UP ABOVE

I don't see why you had to bring the cat. It smells awful."

Ms. Sparks was in a foul mood as she walked up Fifth Avenue. It was hot and sticky and Mr. Carp's cat really did put off an odor. He'd tried everything — mothballs, kitty baths, perfume — but Claudius was born to stink.

Mr. Carp glanced down at the long-haired feline attached to a ragged leash (Claudius *hated* the leash) and tried to cover for what appeared to be his only friend in the world.

"It's not my fault I can't afford a cat walker," Mr. Carp complained. "Claudius spends all day inside a sweltering apartment; what do you expect?" He was sweating under the rim of a wide sun hat as he tried to keep up with Ms. Sparks, whose long stride was equal to two of his own.

Ms. Sparks crumpled her nose in disgust.

"I'll make Leo Fillmore keep it in the basement. It's the only way."

"But —"

"Silence!" Ms. Sparks said as they approached the vast grounds of the Whippet Hotel. Mr. Carp thought she looked positively mesmerized at the site of the tall iron gate. She gazed into the openness and stood as still as a statue, her heart leaping at the wonder of what lay inside. She wasn't the only one who felt this way. It was common for passersby to gawk at the property as if they'd stumbled onto the edge of the Grand Canyon. With skyscrapers all around its edges, the corner lot where the hotel sat was a gripping sight. Rolling pathways on green grass, giant bushes cut into the shapes of animals, a pond — all with the tiny, miraculous hotel in the middle.

"We meet again," Ms. Sparks said, just above a whisper. The chill in her voice made Mr. Carp shiver even in the hot sun. Claudius tried to climb through one of the openings between the iron bars, but his head was too big. He, too, wanted to go inside. There were small birds and rodents to be chased in there. A cat could get used to a place like this, might even stay outside all summer long, climbing the trees and sleeping in the warm sun by the pond.

"Let me do all the talking," Ms. Sparks warned. Her tall hairdo was casting a shadow over Mr. Carp's face as he removed the silly hat and held it nervously in one of his grease-stained hands. Ms. Sparks loved casting intimidating shadows with her hair.

"Do you understand?" Ms. Sparks asked, her crooked finger hovering over the call button that would, more than likely, lead to an open gate. She was worried about how Mr. Yancey would take to Mr. Carp and his awful cat. "You're here to observe, Mr. Carp, to make it official. Nothing more. The less you talk, the better."

Mr. Carp seethed inside. Who did she think she was, the queen of England? But he was, to all appearances, a desperate man with no backbone. The Whippet was the answer, and Ms. Sparks the way in. All he really wanted was for her to stop glaring at him.

And so he nodded. *Of course, this is your show. I'm only here to observe.*

Ms. Sparks smiled an evil, sharp-toothed grin and pushed the gate button, which buzzed annoyingly against her finger.

"Whippet Hotel, state your business," a voice crackled. In the absence of Pilar and Remi and Leo, LillyAnn Pompadore had taken a break. The front desk was being manned by Captain Rickenbacker. He had no idea what he was doing and, besides, he was playing checkers with Mr. Phipps.

"It's Ms. Sparks. Let me in. I have business to discuss."

"Oh! Uhhhhhhhh," Captain Rickenbacker said. He looked at Mr. Phipps, not knowing what to do.

"I'm afraid you're not allowed on the property," Mr. Phipps answered, somewhat feebly. He had always been terrified of Ms. Sparks when she'd been in charge of the hotel.

"Rickenbacker! And you, Phipps!" she yelled into the speaker. People who had been hovering near the gate outside began moving away, uncomfortable with where this was going. "I know it's you two in there. Don't deny it."

"No, no, we would never . . ." Mr. Phipps trailed off. Captain Rickenbacker was already halfway to the stairs on the way to his room. Like most superheroes, he preferred playing pinball to being yelled at.

"Listen *good*, you two," Ms. Sparks fumed. "Open. This. Gate. And get Mr. Yancey. Tell him to meet me in the lobby."

No one responded. Captain Rickenbacker had fled and Mr. Phipps was seriously contemplating an escape of his own to the garden shed.

"OPEN THE GATE!"

Mr. Carp tugged on Claudius's mangled leash and started backing away quietly.

"Where do you think you're going?" Ms. Sparks said without taking her eyes off the hotel. She waited impatiently as Claudius sat down and licked the matted fur on his right foot.

When the gate buzzed softly, Ms. Sparks glowed with excitement. She knew that sound, knew what it meant. The gate was unlocked, and she pushed it open, stepping onto the soft grass on the other side and fixing her narrow eyes on the mysterious hotel in the distance. Her whole body tingled.

Just you wait, Merganzer D. Whippet, she thought. *Soon this will all be mine.*

"Come," she said, waving Mr. Carp forward without looking at him. "You'll like the room I've chosen for you. Much better than that cave you've been living in all these years."

Mr. Carp looked back in the direction of the crummy neighborhood they'd walked from. He could run, even leave Claudius behind if he had to. But, for many complicated reasons, he did not run. His moment had come and it would never come again. He turned and passed through the gate with Claudius leading the way. When he heard the iron clang behind him, he knew his fate was sealed.

There would be no turning back now.

***

And so it was that when Leo and Remi returned to the lobby expecting to find Ms. Pompadore, they found their old nemesis instead. Ms. Sparks had taken up residence in precisely the same place from which she'd run the hotel with an iron fist for years: behind the registration desk. She was speaking to Mr. Yancey in a small voice, like they were plotting.

"I knew we shouldn't have left LillyAnn Pompadore in charge," whispered Remi from their hiding place inside the duck elevator. They'd opened the door just a crack, hoping Betty didn't quack and give them away. "We leave for a few hours and she loses control of the hotel. Great."

"I'll admit, it's a supersized catastrophe," Leo said. "I'm fairly speechless."

Leo thought of how disappointed his dad and Pilar and Merganzer would be. They'd left him in charge and the one person who could ruin everything had found her way into the hotel in less than a day. It was a disaster.

Leo was trying to think of a plan when he heard a noise. It was soft and fuzzy at the edge of his hearing. At first he thought it was Betty, snoring quietly. But when he looked at Remi, he knew it wasn't Betty. Remi had one of the easiest faces in the world to read. When he was hiding something, his dark eyebrows went up and the middle of his forehead crinkled. He'd heard the sound, too, and it had worried him.

"You didn't," Leo said.

Leo pulled the small duck elevator door all the way shut and stared at his brother.

"Didn't do what?" Remi asked, his eyebrows raising, his forehead crinkling. "I don't know what you're talking about."

"What if she gets loose? Then what are we going to do?" Leo asked.

"But she won't. I'll make sure," Remi said. He knew immediately he'd given himself away.

Loopa peeked slowly out of Remi's red jacket pocket. The little monkey had woken up. She was cute when she woke up, groggy-eyed and yawning. It was impossible not to smile.

"I couldn't leave her there," Remi explained, petting the little monkey on her furry head. Loopa smiled up at him. "We bonded."

"Just don't give her any Flart's Fizz. She'd blow our cover for sure."

"She'll be quiet, won't you?" Remi said. But when Remi looked, the monkey had fallen back to sleep.

"See? No worries," Remi said.

Leo wasn't so sure, but he gently pulled the doors open again. Betty got right up close to Loopa with her orange bill and stared curiously. She was acting motherly. It was what she did.

"Keep them both quiet," Leo said, putting his finger to his lips. It wasn't as if Remi could stop Betty from quacking or Loopa from making monkey sounds if they wanted to, but Leo still hoped for silence as he peered out into the lobby.

It was hard to hear what they were saying, but he definitely heard some things that alarmed him.

Mr. Yancey: "Who's the new guy, and what's with the cat?"

Ms. Sparks: "Don't worry about them, just be ready."

Mr. Yancey: "I can't believe our luck. It's too perfect."

Ms. Sparks: "Where are those boys? They make me nervous."

"What are they saying?" Remi whispered. He was getting tired of sitting in the cramped duck elevator and wanted to get out. Betty was looking at him like she might start quacking at any moment.

"They're in it together, Yancey and Ms. Sparks," Leo explained.

"In *what* together?" asked Remi.

"That's exactly what I'm going to find out. Take Betty to the roof as fast as you can, and I'll meet you back here. I'm getting to the bottom of this."

"But —"

Remi wasn't sure it was a great idea to talk to Ms. Sparks, but Leo was the official owner of the hotel. Technically Remi was just the bellboy and the doorman, and in this particular situation, he was glad. It was a good moment not to be responsible.

Leo quietly opened the duck elevator door and crept out into the hall next to the lobby. The doors shut and Remi, Loopa, and Betty were gone, slowly rising toward the roof. Leo put on his most confident face, straightened his Whippet Hotel maintenance overalls, and started for the lobby. He passed through, toward the main doors, as if he hadn't even noticed Ms. Sparks or Mr. Yancey.

"Leo Fillmore," Ms. Sparks said. Her voice was full of satisfaction, like she was enjoying the fact that she'd appeared with bad news and it would surprise him to see her.

"Oh, hi, Ms. Sparks," Leo said. "Did you need something? Because I'm kind of busy right at the moment." Leo nodded in Mr. Yancey's direction. "I hope your stay is going well, Mr. Yancey. We always appreciate your visits."

Ms. Sparks looked quickly back and forth between Leo and Mr. Yancey, as if she'd been momentarily stunned into silence. It didn't last long.

"I do have a rather pressing matter to discuss, if it's not too much of a bother."

She leaned over the desk in Leo's general direction as Mr. Yancey's phone rang. He used it as an excuse to leave the lobby, waving at Leo indifferently as he passed by.

"Come to think of it," Leo said, rubbing his chin as if he'd only just remembered an important fact, "you're banned from the hotel grounds."

"Oh, that." Ms. Sparks smiled. "I don't think it's going to be a problem. You see, I've got permission."

"Permission from whom?" Leo walked two steps closer to Ms. Sparks. This was getting interesting, and not in a good way.

Ms. Sparks held up a letter and began reading aloud.

"'By the power vested in me, I do hereby appoint Ms. Lenora Sparks the Tax Evasion Specialist for the Whippet Hotel and its associated properties. Ms. Sparks is granted state authority to oversee this matter during the twenty-four hours after the signing of this letter. During that time, she is to observe, in person, the goings-on at said property. No items of value are to be removed.'"

There was more, but Ms. Sparks stopped reading. She felt she'd read enough to make her point.

"It goes on, but it only gets worse."

Leo reached into the front pocket of his overalls feeling a little better. If this was about taxes, he'd already solved the problem. This was going to be easier than he'd thought.

"You need seven hundred thousand dollars. I know all about it. Fortunately, I've already prepared the necessary payment."

He had no intention of letting Ms. Sparks touch the note, or even get within two feet of it. Instead, he held it out so she could see it, then yanked it back and held it tight in his hand.

"It will be couriered directly to the proper authorities before the close of business today," Leo continued. He thought he'd done a fine job of sounding like he knew what he was doing. In reality, he didn't actually know who to give the note to, but he was sure Mr. Phipps would.

"Oh, my dear boy," said Ms. Sparks, and this time she pretended to actually care. "You've been misinformed.

Let me guess — Merganzer left you holding the bag? You can't trust *him*. I tried to warn you. He's no good with numbers, never has been. Always misplacing those pesky zeros."

Leo was confused. "I don't understand. How much do you think the Whippet Hotel owes?"

Ms. Sparks came out from behind the desk, holding the official-looking piece of paper.

"I don't *think*, I know. It's a very serious matter. You're going to lose this hotel, Leo Fillmore. There's simply no doubt about it."

She glanced at the contract once more, just to be sure.

"This hotel is seven *million* dollars behind on its debt to the great state of New York. They have tried to reach you, but you have not answered their letters."

This was not entirely true. The fact was, Ms. Sparks had been intercepting the letters for many months. It was all part of her diabolical plan.

Leo was in a daze. Seven *million*? Before he realized it, Ms. Sparks had come nearer and snatched the seven hundred thousand dollar note out of his hand.

"This will do just fine as a down payment, but I'm afraid you're still six million, three hundred thousand short. And did I mention I was given this authority eighteen hours ago? Maybe I didn't. You're down to six hours, Leo Fillmore. Better get cracking."

She leaned in so that her nose nearly touched Leo's. Ms. Sparks could be an extremely close talker when she felt in charge.

"I almost feel sorry for you, having to run this hotel on your own. You'll be better off without it."

"I don't believe you," Leo said, but he was shaking. Could she really take the hotel from him, just like that?

She stood up straight and stared down at Leo.

"It doesn't matter if you believe it or not, it's true. Eighteen of your precious hours have already passed. You have six hours to come up with the rest, and we both know that's not going to happen."

Leo started to back away, and then he had a thought.

"What's Mr. Yancey got to do with this?" he asked.

"That's none of your business!" she yelled. Ms. Sparks pocketed the seven hundred thousand dollar note and brushed a duck feather off her shoulder with a sour face. "And when I own this hotel, there will be no ducks. I won't be running a zoo with monkeys and birds and who knows what else!"

Ms. Sparks didn't know how right she was.

"Stay close by in case I need you," she went on. "And don't even think about leaving the hotel. I've assigned a guardian for you, since your parents are gone and everyone else in this hotel is stark raving mad!"

"A guardian?"

"He's waiting for you in that hovel you call a room. He's not to let you out of his sight. It's one thing — the *only* thing — he happens to be good at. He knows how to keep track of someone when the need arises."

Leo didn't like the sound of a guardian one bit, especially one who had a weird super-ability to keep an eye on people. It would greatly complicate things if he and Remi were to make it back under the hotel and find the things Merganzer needed. He hadn't counted on all this trouble and wished his dad were there to help him.

Remi hadn't returned in the duck waiter when Leo passed by, and he needed to get Blop from the basement room. The world felt like it was falling apart as he walked the steps down to the basement door.

"Ew," he said, crinkling his nose. He hadn't even gone inside and already he could smell Claudius. When he entered the basement, it reeked of wet cat fur. A small, unhappy-looking man was sitting on his bed holding a wadded up cat leash in his hand. His skin was pale, he had a thick, drooping mustache, and there were large bags under his eyes. There was a frailness about him, like a soft summer breeze might knock him over.

"You must be the guardian," Leo said. Mr. Carp was staring at the call center wall where Daisy, the mechanical shark who delivered commands from the hotel guests, was quietly resting.

"Claudius doesn't like your shark," Mr. Carp said. "It makes him nervous."

"If it's any consolation, Daisy makes me nervous, too. You never know when she's going to wake up and deliver bad news."

"I see," Mr. Carp said. The cat meowed and rubbed up against Leo's leg, leaving a trail of fur behind on his overalls.

"I'm Mr. Carp. And this is Claudius," Mr. Carp said, pointing down at the cat.

"I see," Leo said, for he had no idea what else *to* say.

"She asked me to keep an eye on you and the other one — Remi, is it? You'll need to stay close by."

"What happens if we don't?" Leo asked, uncertain how much power Mr. Carp actually had.

Mr. Carp shrugged his shoulders as if he didn't really care.

"Will it be all right if I use the extra bunk while I'm visiting?" Mr. Carp asked, looking at Clarence Fillmore's empty bed. "I think this is what Ms. Sparks had in mind. It's very nice down here. Much nicer than my apartment."

The basement was cozy for a maintenance man and his son, with its glugging water heater and hotel parts everywhere, but it was by any reasonable standard a crummy place for a normal person to live. Leo could only imagine what sort of place Mr. Carp rented.

"You can stay — just don't touch anything," Leo said. He felt sorry for Mr. Carp, but at the same time, he was feeling a little better about things. There was no way this guardian would be able to keep track of Leo and Remi. Things were looking up.

Mr. Carp reclined on Leo's dad's bed and Claudius jumped up next to him. This, Leo knew, meant he'd have to burn the bedding when the cat was gone.

"Remember, no leaving the hotel," Mr. Carp said, and then he closed his eyes. Leo didn't move for a full minute, during which Mr. Carp began to snore lightly and Claudius coughed up a hairball that landed with a wet sound on the concrete floor.

"Pssssst!"

Remi had entered the basement and stood at the bottom of the stairs holding his nose. Loopa was sitting on Remi's shoulder, digging a monkey finger into Remi's ear.

"Shhhh," Leo whispered as quietly as he could. He walked to his bed, got down on his knees, and fished his hand around in search of Blop. A moment later, he and Remi were standing together at the door, the little robot safely deposited in Remi's red jacket.

"That monkey is going to be trouble," Leo said as he watched it run up and down the entire length of Remi's body.

"Yeah, she definitely woke up," Remi said. "At least she's quiet."

Loopa was an especially quiet monkey, but as Leo watched her leap off of Remi's shoulder and land on the floor, he could see it was going to be difficult to control her.

"Who's the smelly dude?" Remi whispered as he picked up Loopa and put her back in his pocket. He had Blop, who was still sleeping, in one pocket, and Loopa in the other. Leo rolled his eyes and started up the stairs, grabbing Remi by the arm and dragging him out of the room. In seconds they were near the lobby, which Ms. Sparks appeared to have left.

"Yeah, she's in my mom's old room," Remi said, unable to hide his loathing. "I hope she's not pulling down all the decorations."

"Come on, I have an idea," Leo said. He ran through the lobby with Remi close behind. On the other side was the Puzzle Room, where piles of puzzle pieces lay on a long, wooden table. There were eight hundred thousand pieces. Mr. Phipps and Captain Rickenbacker were fond of trying to put it together, but had never gotten very far.

"I wish you could have seen it when Merganzer made the pieces fly everywhere," Leo told Remi, smiling at the memory. "That was something else."

He took a black key card out of one of the side pockets of his maintenance overalls. He knew how to work the card so the piles of puzzle pieces would fly into the air and miraculously settle into the finished picture they were meant to be. Merganzer had showed him how to do it.

"Only to be used when the time is right," Leo said out loud. "Remember what I told you Merganzer said about the puzzle being double-sided?"

"Two sides," Remi said. "I remember."

After Merganzer had left last time, Leo had taken the puzzle apart again, leaving it in piles on the table. Putting it back together was an almost impossible task without the black key card.

"Should I do it?" Leo asked, his thumb hovering over the card, ready to swipe back and forth in the way that would send the pieces flying. He could put it together, build it so they could see the other side, a side they'd never seen before.

"I don't know — does it seem like the right time?" Remi asked.

Leo couldn't be sure, but there was one thing he *was* sure of: He *would* know when the time was right.

He put the key card away and shrugged. "I don't think it's time," he said.

Remi was having some trouble keeping Loopa in his pocket. He kept having to hold her head down while her arms snaked out in a desperate attempt to free herself.

Just then, out of nowhere, the sound of a gigantic burp echoed through the lobby and into the Puzzle Room. It lasted a full ten seconds.

"Remi," Leo said, concern rising in his voice.

"Uh-huh."

"Where's that bottle of Flart's Fizz?"

Blop's mechanical eyes began to flutter. The little robot was waking up. He was sitting in the jacket pocket where the bottle had been.

"I left it in the duck elevator," Remi said. "I thought it would be safe there."

"Lovely day, don't you think?" Blop said, and Leo knew it was only the very beginning of a long-winded description of the sun, the clouds, the mechanics of a lovely day.

Remi and Leo ran back through the lobby, which was still empty, and arrived at the duck elevator. They were both hoping to find Captain Rickenbacker or Mr. Phipps. Even the other long-stay tenants, LillyAnn Pompadore or Theodore Bump, would have been survivable. But they did not find any of those people trying desperately to open the second (and last) bottle of Flart's Fizz. There was already one empty bottle sitting on its side.

"You took *two* bottles?" Leo asked, looking at Remi like he couldn't believe his brother had not only tricked Ingrid into giving him one, but had also taken an extra!

"It wasn't for me," Remi said, pleading to be understood. "Honest. I thought we could each have, you know, one more big burp."

"It was nice of you to think of me, but really, you shouldn't have."

Remi knew Leo was right. It had felt wrong tricking Ingrid, even worse slipping an extra into his pocket when she wasn't looking. But seeing Jane Yancey with the last bottle of Flart's Fizz was too much.

"Put that down, you little thief!" Remi yelled.

Remi should have known better than to cross Jane Yancey. She was spectacularly spoiled, prone to hitting first and yelling right after.

"Get back!" she yelled, hugging the last full bottle of Flart's Fizz to her chest as she crawled all the way inside the duck elevator and started pushing buttons.

Leo calmly put his foot against the door so it wouldn't close and crouched down next to her, blocking the way out.

"Hi, Jane. How's it going?" he asked. It was best to talk calmly to a cornered monster.

"You can't have it!" she yelled. "It's mine! I found it fair and square!"

"You're not even allowed in there, you little creep!" Remi said. He'd gotten down on one knee, reaching in toward the bottle. "Do you have any idea how rare those bottles are? And you already drank one without even asking!"

"I'll tell my dad, I will," she hissed. "He'll be very interested in this stuff, whatever it is. Best burp EVER!"

"I know, right?" Remi said. For a brief instant he was overcome with excitement about the fizzy drink and wanted to talk about it and remember what it was like and . . .

"Remi, please," Leo said. Then he turned to Jane. "We really do need you to give it back. How about a dollar?"

Jane was trying desperately to open the second bottle with her hand, but it wasn't a twist-off. She laughed in Leo's face — money meant nothing to Jane Yancey, she had all she needed and more — and then she put the end of the bottle in her mouth, which apparently was how she'd gotten the first one open.

"Get your disgusting mouth off my bottle of Flart's Fizz!" Remi yelled, lunging for the bottle. Jane Yancey screamed — and, boy, could she wail when she wanted to. Leo could see the entire situation was rapidly spinning out of control. He didn't know what else to do. There was only one thing he could think of that might get her to stop screaming at the top of her lungs, ruining everything.

"How about a monkey?" Leo said. "Would you trade me the bottle for a monkey?"

Remi looked at Leo like he'd lost his marbles. He was so shocked, it turned him speechless. His face, the color of a perfectly toasted marshmallow, turned two shades whiter.

"You did not just say that," Remi finally said.

Jane Yancey had gone silent, taking the end of the bottle out of her mouth. There was slobber all over the bottle cap, but it was still on. She hadn't managed to pry it off with her teeth.

"*You* have a monkey?" she said. "What do you take me for, a complete idiot?"

But there was doubt in her voice. It was, after all, the Whippet Hotel. It was full of surprises. Only seconds ago she'd produced the miracle burp of a lifetime. Maybe there was a monkey somewhere nearby.

Blop began talking about monkeys. Loopa, who had been scared and therefore very quiet up to that point, peeked her head out from the other red jacket pocket.

"There are two hundred sixty-four different species of monkeys," Blop said, but Jane Yancey was suddenly and irreversibly mesmerized by Loopa. Blop went on and on about marmosets and night monkeys and howlers and spider monkeys.

"Put a sock in it, robot," Jane Yancey said, reaching toward Loopa. Loopa made a ridiculously cute gurgling sound and Jane Yancey cackled like a hyena.

"I must have it! I *will* have it!" she said, laughing.

"The monkey for the bottle and your complete silence," Leo said. Remi could not believe his ears. Was Leo really giving Loopa away? It couldn't be. He was heartbroken.

Jane Yancey looked at the bottle of Flart's Fizz and thought about how good it had tasted, better than anything she'd drunk in her life. And that burp. That glorious burp! It was pure magic.

Still, it was a monkey, and not just any monkey: a tiny, goofy, silly monkey, small enough to put her doll clothes on.

"Here," she finally said. "Take your stupid bottle of pop. But first give me the monkey."

"There's just one rule," Leo said, "and you have to promise me you'll follow it."

"I hate rules," Jane said.

"It's just, well, this is a rare monkey. *Super* rare. So rare that there are certain people in this hotel who might want to take her from you."

"Ms. Sparks?" Jane Yancey asked. She was starting to come around.

"Yes! Ms. Sparks! And not to be too harsh, but I think maybe your dad, too. I mean, he's really into money, right? He might want to sell Loopa if he finds out."

"*Sell* my monkey?" Jane Yancey said. Her heart was starting to melt for the little monkey in Remi's pocket. "But he *can't* sell my monkey!"

"Exactly!" Leo said. He heard someone in the lobby, around the corner where he couldn't see, and brought down his voice. "Which is why you need to keep the monkey in the Flying Farm Room. No one goes in there, so it'll be safe, right?"

"Right," she said. Jane Yancey smiled at Leo and made her best yucky face at Remi, both in the space of a second. She was lightning fast with facial expressions.

Leo and Remi piled into the duck elevator next to Jane. It was a tight fit, and as they climbed the floors up to the Flying Farm Room, Remi reluctantly took Loopa out of his pocket.

"Her name is Loopa," Remi said. "Be nice to her, okay?"

"I'm the nicest person I know, fatso!"

Remi grabbed the bottle of Flart's Fizz and wanted to open it, guzzle it, and mega-burp in Jane Yancey's face. He was barely overweight to begin with, like twenty pounds. And he'd actually lost a few since he'd last seen this little jerk sitting in front of him.

But he could see that Leo had been right. Jane Yancey melted into a gross puddle of girly sweetness the second Loopa landed in her lap. There was no way Jane Yancey would let anyone near Loopa. Loopa tried to squirm free, but Jane held the little monkey close and cooed at it, which calmed Loopa down.

"Remember, only the Flying Farm Room," Leo said. "It's not safe anywhere else."

"No problem," Jane said. Loopa curled up in her lap and made soft monkey sounds, which sent Jane into a tizzy fit of giggles.

When they arrived at the floor of the Flying Farm Room, Leo and Remi walked her to the door and unlocked it.

"I'll let you keep the key card, but only if you promise not to let her out. And you have to feed her, you know, monkey food."

Leo looked at Remi, who shrugged. Neither of them knew what to feed a monkey.

"I'll figure it out," Jane Yancey said, and just like that, she snatched up the key card, passed through the door, and slammed it in their faces.

"You do have another key card for that room, right?" Remi asked. "Because eventually we'll need to rescue my monkey from the clutches of that evil princess."

As if on cue, both boys heard Jane Yancey yell from the other side of the door: "Rip-off! This monkey has no tail!"

"Come on, let's get out of here fast," Leo said.

They'd picked up Blop and dropped off a hyper monkey, but there was still work to be done before their fateful encounter with Dr. Flart.

They had to find out where to put the zip rope, otherwise known as Loopa's tail.

And they'd need to do it while avoiding Mr. Carp, Ms. Sparks, and finding six million, three hundred thousand dollars.

CHAPTER 5

AN ISLE OF PENGUINS, A BOY NAMED TWIST, ROBINSON CRUSOE!

Leo and Remi stood in the Whippet Library. It was on the hidden thirteenth floor, and there was only one way of getting there: the silver key card. Leo kept this card, which unlocked every door in the hotel, on a chain around his neck. It was the only silver card in existence, so he was sure Ms. Sparks would have loved to get her hands on it.

"Quite a ride," Remi said. His hair was standing on end and his stomach didn't feel so good.

"It's the only way in," Leo said.

The silver key card unlocked a panel in the duck elevator, which revealed four buttons that had to be pushed in just the right order. Doing it right sent the duck elevator on a wild journey back and forth and up and down, ending at the thirteenth floor. Leo left the one and only fuse they had in their possession in the duck elevator for safekeeping. He knew things might get wacky in the library and didn't want to risk breaking it.

"What did he say again?" Remi asked. "Penguin twisting desert island, or something like that?"

"Your brain works in mysterious ways," Leo said, and it was true. Remi wasn't right, but he was kind of close. Leo corrected him. "An isle of Penguins, a boy named Twist, and Robinson Crusoe."

"That's what I said," Remi concluded seriously. And he had, only in not so many words.

"You're right about one thing: *Robinson Crusoe* is about a guy stranded on a desert island. Twist must be *Oliver Twist*. The Penguin has me stumped."

They spent the next few minutes looking through Merganzer's vast collection of books. The volumes ran floor to ceiling on twenty-feet-tall shelves, snaking in every direction, and Remi insisted on being the one to ride the ladder while Leo pushed it.

"To the left, another few feet," Remi said as they searched for the Charles Dickens section. Leo pushed the ladder, which rolled on wheels connected to the floor and ceiling, until Remi told him to stop.

"Got it!" Remi said, pulling out the book. He stood on the ladder waiting for something to happen, but nothing did.

"As I suspected," Leo said. "That's the second book we're supposed to find, not the first."

They didn't know what the Penguin book was, so they searched for *Robinson Crusoe*, even though it wasn't the first book, either.

"Got it!" Remi yelled.

Leo thought he heard a familiar sound behind him, but he wasn't sure.

"Was that —"

"Coming down!" Remi yelled before Leo could finish. Remi liked the idea of sliding down a ladder like it was a fire station pole. He let his feet flop to the sides and slid down with only his hands. It turned out that actually using a ladder like a sliding pole was not as fun as the idea of doing it. Within the first five feet, his hands were on fire, the friction burning hot against his skin like a supercharged rug burn. He tried to get his feet back on the rungs, which sent his legs flying wildly in every direction, like hail ricocheting against pavement.

He landed hard, barely missing Leo, but somehow managed only a few scrapes and bruises.

"Let's hope the Penguin is closer to the ground," Leo said. "And also, I'm going up this time. You're scaring me."

Leo started climbing the narrow ladder for a look around and quickly found himself twenty rungs up.

"Let's check the card catalog; maybe it will help," Remi yelled with a snap of his fingers.

Merganzer D. Whippet wasn't exactly antitechnology, but he did like to have everything written down in case whatever computer he was using went on the fritz. With the Whippet Library, he always kept the entire collection in a card catalog system organized in various ways. There were at least three cards for every book, because he found that sometimes he was searching for a writer, sometimes a title, and sometimes a subject.

Searching through authors was no help at all, so Remi knew pretty quickly that the writer's name was not Penguin. Searching through the subject revealed a healthy selection of titles having to do with penguin life, but he came up empty-handed after searching through them all for something about an "isle of Penguins."

"This is taking a long time," Leo yelled down, frustrated and hungry. They hadn't eaten all day. "Maybe we should take a break and get some animal crackers."

Normally, this would have been an immediately agreeable idea for Remi, but he'd started searching through the title card catalog and finally hit pay dirt.

"*Penguin Island*!" Remi shouted, holding up the card and waving it around like he'd won the lottery. "I found it!"

Leo started climbing down, but halfway to the bottom Remi began pushing the ladder so fast, Leo lost his grip with one hand and spiraled out into the air.

"It's by a French guy named France," Remi said, lurching to a stop where he thought the book might be. Remi had discovered the writer named France was French because Merganzer D. Whippet had noted this fact on the card — a very Merganzer thing to do.

Leo spun back around and banged his knees on a ladder rung, but at least he had both hands attached again. He was safe, for the moment.

"Did you not hear me screaming up here?" Leo yelled.

"I know, right? I'm excited, too!" Remi called up.

"Let me know when you're going to push the ladder that hard next time, will you?" Leo asked. He was going to tell Remi about nearly falling to his death, but Remi spooked easily. Better to just let it pass.

"By the looks of this number, *Penguin Island* is way up there, near the ceiling," Remi said. "Should be right here, straight up."

Leo looked up. It was the tallest section of the library, right next to the pond on the roof, which had the most amazing glass bottom. He could see the ducks swimming around in the mottled late afternoon sunlight.

"Are you sure?" Leo asked. He didn't really want to go all the way up there with Remi holding the ladder.

"Yeah, I'm pretty sure. Like, seventy percent sure."

"Tell me if you're going to move the ladder, okay?" Leo pleaded.

"Check!" Remi said, and gave a solute.

"I can verify the information," Blop said. He'd gotten a look at the card, which Remi had shoved in his jacket pocket. "Mr. Whippet and I spent many hours creating the card system. Very complicated business, lots of logic involved. You see, the way it works is you start with the writer and cross reference the subject with the title. . . ."

Leo completely tuned out Blop's small mechanical voice as it echoed through the grand library space. He climbed, fast and with purpose, until his head was nearly touching the ceiling. He could tell by looking back and forth that he was very near the center of the room. When he looked at Remi, he realized how high up he was, and it took his breath away.

"Grab the book," Remi said. "The sooner we get this done, the sooner we can get back in the elevator."

Leo found the spine for *Penguin Island*. The author was on the spine, too: *France*. Pulling out the book, Leo hoped there wouldn't be some sort of explosion that would knock him off the ladder, but he didn't need to worry. Absolutely nothing happened.

"This is ridiculous," Leo said, irritated with Merganzer's crazy way of hiding things. But peering into the space where the book had been, Leo saw another book hidden in the shadows. He pulled out four or five books on each side and dropped them to the floor. It rained books, and Leo felt bad. Not for Remi, who was unsuccessfully dodging about half of them, but because the books were being damaged on the way down.

"Try to catch them!" Leo yelled, but he wasn't really paying attention to what was happening down below. He was laser-focused on the copy of *Oliver Twist* that was standing alone between two slabs of marble. It was a hardback edition, thick and old.

"I think I'm figuring it out," Leo called to Remi.

"Great. Maybe warn me if you're going to keep throwing books. A guy wants to be prepared."

But there were no more books to throw. Leo pulled out the copy of *Oliver Twist* and set it gently in the space he'd created by removing other, less important books.

And there it was.

All alone, deep in the dark shadow of the library, a single book stood hidden.

"I think I found it!" Leo said.

Leo took a deep breath and reached back into the darkness. It crossed his mind that there might be spiders or mice or rats in the darkest part of an old library, and he hadn't actually seen what the book was. It was too dark for that. Still, he gathered his courage, reached all the way in up to his shoulder, and took the spine in his hand.

And then he pulled.

"I got it! It is the right book," Leo yelled down. "It's *Robinson Crusoe*!"

Leo waited for something to happen, but nothing did. He began to think maybe he was supposed to do something with the book and started flipping through its pages.

"Um, Leo?" Remi said.

"Ah, you've set things in motion. Very exciting," Blop said, and then he went on about the mechanics of how the shelves were moving. Unfortunately for Leo, he wasn't really listening to Blop, and Remi was nearly speechless.

"This book is past due," Leo said, shaking his head and wondering why it was hidden in a secret place. He had one arm hooked through the ladder as he came to the last page. "It's not even Merganzer's book. He checked it out from the Brooklyn Public Library twenty-three years ago and never returned it."

"Leo," Remi said, finally getting his voice back. "Hold on!"

Leo closed the book and looked down, wondering what the problem was. But before he could get a good look, Remi shoved the ladder as hard as he could. This time, Leo couldn't hold on.

He was falling, and the only thing that was going to save him were the shelves of books that were flying past. Leo dropped the copy of *Robinson Crusoe* and reached out, grabbing the ledge of a shelf full of books about polar bears, whales, and sea creatures. The impact stretched Leo's arms to the breaking point, then he let go and caught the next ledge down. He was going slower the second time, and held firm.

"Get out of the way, Leo!" Remi shouted.

Leo looked down and saw his legs hanging limply in the air. He was losing his grip, but that wasn't the worse part of his predicament. The shelves below him were spinning like revolving doors. Ten-feet-high sections, starting at the floor, were whirling in circles as if stuck to a pole in a furious wind.

And the spinning sections of bookshelves were getting closer.

Leo was nearly forty feet in the air. But two ten-feet-high sections were already spinning, and the section right below him was starting to move. He didn't have much time before the section of shelf he was hanging from would start spinning, too.

"Try to climb down!" Remi yelled. But the ladder had been pushed off to the side and the spinning shelves weren't going to let it back in.

"But how?!" Leo yelled. He glanced down as three of his four fingers on each hand pulled away.

I can time this just right, Leo said to himself. *I can do it.*

The shelf Leo was holding on to began to move, and as it did, Leo let go with his last fingers. He landed with a thud on the turning shelf below, and slid off to the side, nearly falling all the way to the hard floor of the library. Just as he was about to be knocked in the head by the shelf above, he dropped once more, landing on the top edge of the second highest spinning shelf.

"You're doing it!" Remi said, clapping his hands together in excitement.

"I know, right?" Leo smiled, but he should have been watching while he was celebrating. The shelf above him came around and knocked him off his feet. He tumbled down, landed hard on the first spinning shelf, then dropped the final ten feet like a bag of flour, knocking Remi over.

Both boys crawled out of the way as Blop began talking about the book Leo had found.

"First book in the Whippet Library, *Robinson Crusoe*," Blop said. Leo was just happy to be alive, and Remi was extremely glad his brother and best friend was okay.

"Second book, *Oliver Twist*. Third book —"

"Let me guess," Remi said. *"Penguin Island?"*

"Third book, *Penguin Island*. Fourth book, *The Hunchback of Notre-Dame*. Fifth book . . ."

"Can you set him on the floor while we check this out?" Leo asked. "There are thousands of books in here. He could be at this awhile."

Remi nodded his agreement and set Blop on the floor, where he happily recited the names and the order of the books that had become part of the collection of the Whippet Library.

"I think we'll need to be careful," Remi said. "Do you have the zip rope?"

Leo patted his hand on one of the side pockets of his maintenance overalls. "Got it."

All the shelves were still spinning, including the bottom one, but not so fast that they couldn't slip through as the opening appeared. Once they reached the other side they found stairs leading down into darkness.

"I don't understand this hotel at all," Leo said. "There must be a hidden floor here, one no one knows about."

At the bottom of the stairs, the boys stopped abruptly, for they had stumbled onto something that looked extremely fragile.

"Don't move," Leo said.

"Dude, this is the coolest thing I've ever seen," Remi said, which was saying a lot, given all the rooms in the Whippet Hotel. "We have to make it go."

On the vast floor before them were thousands upon thousands of dominoes. They wound all through the space, up and down long ramps, through silver rings, under bridges of stone. In the very center of the room sat a safe, and on top of the safe, a golden duck.

"He does like himself a good duck," Remi observed.

"I wonder how it all works," Leo said.

"Easy, you just push one over and the whole things tumbles!" Without asking Leo, Remi touched the toe of his shiny doorman shoe to the edge of the very closest domino.

"No, don't!" Leo warned, covering his eyes at the thought of having to set all the dominoes back up again if it didn't work.

"Hey," Remi said, touching the first domino again. "It's not moving." Remi tapped the domino a little harder. Then he kicked it. Then he jumped on top of a whole bunch of standing dominoes.

None of them moved.

"Interesting," Leo observed, kneeling down for a closer look. "They're metal, and so is the floor."

"Heaviest dominoes I ever saw," Remi said, but Leo thought he knew the truth.

"It's like the puzzle downstairs. The floor is a giant magnet holding them all perfectly still."

"Merganzer is awesome," Remi said, shaking his head at such a wacky invention.

They both traveled through the maze of dominoes and stood in front of the safe, which had a handle of weathered wood. Leo tried opening it, but it was shut tight, and there was no dial or lock. He also noticed a strange humming sound in the air, like the sound of many bees high in a tree.

"Has to be the dominoes," Leo said. "There must be a way to make them move."

"Number eighty-seven, *The Cat in the Hat*," Blop said. "A personal favorite."

The little robot had rolled up to the edge of the stairs. He was looking down at them with his bright mechanical eyes.

"Blop," Leo called, walking back toward the stairs and leaving Remi to stare at the golden duck, "do you know how to make the dominoes move?"

"Number eighty-eight," Blop said, but then he stopped, having been given a different directive. "Why yes, I *do* know how to make the dominoes move. It's fun to watch. Would you like to move them?"

"I would," Leo said.

"Pull the duck's leg."

Leo looked back at Remi, who already had his hand on the narrow leg of the golden duck.

"Like this?" Remi asked, and he pulled. The leg came up and the humming sound disappeared.

"Cool," Remi said. He backed up two steps, letting go of the leg, and accidentally touched the heel of his shoe against a random metal domino. It fell over, knocking down other dominoes in their turn.

"Must be done in the right order, or the emergency lock will engage," Blop said. "Only Merganzer can open it if that happens."

The dominoes were falling fast, racing around the room with incredible speed. "We have to stop it before it's too late!" Leo cried.

Remi took this to mean that he should dive onto the moving dominoes and try to stop them, which was funny to watch but not very helpful. He dove from section to section, trying to bring things to a halt, but dominoes kept falling all around him.

"Blop," Leo said, staring up at the robot at the top of the stairs, "can we stop it?"

"Of course you can."

"Can you tell me how?" Leo asked in his calmest voice. He wanted to freak out, but he knew Blop responded best to direct and simple commands.

"Push the duck's leg back down."

This time it was Leo running through the room, knocking down dominoes with almost every step he took. By the time he reached the golden duck, about ninety percent of all the dominoes had fallen. He pushed the golden leg back down and heard the humming sound return. Like magic, every domino jumped back to its starting position, all standing at attention like thousands of rectangular army men.

"Whew," Remi said. "That was a close call."

Leo stayed where he was and sent Remi back to the stairs, where he waited for Leo to pull the golden duck leg up again. When he did, Remi tapped the first domino. Leo and Remi got to watch as every last one fell in perfect order: up ramps, under bridges, through rings that had lit up with fire.

Near the end, the dominoes toppled up a long ramp that ended above the safe. The last domino fell, landing directly on the duck. There was a slot on the golden duck's back and the domino fit perfectly inside.

Then the golden duck laid a golden egg, which dropped through a hole on top of the safe.

"It's moving," Remi said, pointing to the duck.

The golden duck began to rise into the air on a long, thin pole. Up it went past the ceiling, to places Leo and Remi couldn't see.

"I think it's on the roof," Leo said, but he couldn't be sure.

He grabbed the wooden handle in front of him and opened Merganzer D. Whippet's safe.

The door was heavy as iron, but it glided on solid brass hinges without a sound. By the time Leo had the safe open, Remi was standing next to him. They both peered in at once.

"There's the egg," Leo said. The golden egg was perched on a stem that looked like a long, silver golf tee. It had landed perfectly. In the center of the safe was a round circle painted in white with a word in the middle:

Fizz.

"Better put the bottle there," Leo said.

Remi took the last bottle of Flart's Fizz out of his red jacket pocket and looked longingly at it one last time. It was orange or brown or sort of yellow inside, he couldn't say. Flart's Fizz was funny like that, a color that was not a color, with the best kind of surprise inside.

"He knows how to hit me where it hurts," Remi said, but he knew it was for the best. It wasn't his bottle of Flart's Fizz.

Remi set the bottle in its place. "This is going really well, don't you think?"

Leo thought about everything they'd already been through in such a short time, how dangerous it had been, and of Ms. Sparks lurking inside his beloved hotel.

"Sure, Remi," he said. "It's going swell. I just hope the second half is easier than the first."

"Don't count on it," Remi said.

Along one side of the safe was a collection of crumpled manila envelopes. The envelopes had the appearance of having been well used, with paint splatters and small notations and schematic drawings in weathered pencil everywhere on their surfaces. Remi pulled one out and found that it had a red wax seal keeping it shut; just like the envelope they'd been given. The seal had a letter *W* pressed into it.

"Looks official," Leo said. "And there are dozens of them. I wonder what's inside."

Remi turned the envelope over and gasped.

"No way."

There were words written there in a wispy, Merganzer D. Whippet style.

Master plans: The Pinball Machine

Leo beamed as he started pulling out envelopes. Each one was crumpled and worn at the edges, full with the sense of having been on location when the real work was happening.

"Remi," Leo whispered. "These are the master plans. It's amazing!"

Leo read two:

Master program and schematic: Blop

Plan model: The Double Helix

"The Double Helix!" Leo yelled. "I LOVE the Double Helix!"

The Double Helix was a secret elevator that ran up the middle of the Whippet Hotel, but really, it was more like the best thrill ride ever. Fast, treacherous, spinning, twisting!

Remi read two more:

Master plan: The Flying Farm Room

The Realm of Gears

And this particular envelope had another note scratched on it, a note that had been written more recently: *Open only when traveling in the Realm of Gears.*

"Whoa, Leo," Remi whispered. "The Realm of Gears. Isn't that one of the places Ingrid said something about?"

"I think you're right," Leo agreed. "It sounds like there are instructions inside."

"But remember what she said: If we needed over a million, we'd have to go there. So we're fine. There's no reason to take the envelope, I guess."

"Actually," Leo said, "I didn't want to worry you, but yeah, we're in some trouble. She wants seven million, not seven hundred thousand."

"Ouch," Remi said. "I don't think selling my comics will get us that far. Or my four bucks."

Both boys thought about what the gears might be like and whether or not the route would be dangerous. They put all the other envelopes away, but kept the one about the Realm of Gears.

"He would have wanted us to have it, right?" Remi said, looking up at Leo for guidance. Leo wasn't older, not really, not enough to matter. But he had always seemed like a barely bigger brother, someone he could trust when he didn't know the answer to a tough problem.

"He's forgetful, for sure," Leo said. "Maybe he meant to say we should take it. He didn't say not to."

That was all the convincing Remi needed. He liked the idea of having some insurance in case things went sideways underground. Folding the envelope the long way, Remi stuffed it in his inside jacket pocket for safekeeping.

They asked Blop how to close the safe, and the little robot explained about the golden egg, how to put it back into the golden duck, and how to close the safe again so it would open when they came back.

"But we'd have to go to the roof to do that," Leo said. "That duck is all the way up there now, at the end if this pole. We don't have time for that now, not with Ms. Sparks threatening to auction off the hotel in about five hours."

They'd made a little bit of a mess, but there was no time to pick up all the fallen books and put everything back the way it was. In fact, there was no time to stop the shelves from turning, even though Blop was determined to tell them the complicated way in which it should be done.

Instead, they ran through the Whippet Library, newly excited by the places they would need to explore in order to finish what they'd started.

The first thing Leo noticed when he returned to the duck elevator was the item that was no longer there.

CHAPTER 6

THE TRAPDOOR CLOSES

I t's gone," Leo said.

"What's gone?" Remi asked.

"The fuse, and it's the only one we have. We can't get back under the hotel without it."

"Did you hear that?" Remi asked.

"Hear what?" Leo asked back.

Someone had used the trapdoor on top of the duck elevator and was still sitting up there, Remi was sure of it. He pointed to the ceiling of the small space.

"Put Blop away before he starts talking," Leo whispered in his smallest voice.

"Who's up there?" Remi shouted without thinking, blowing their cover as Leo slapped his forehead in frustration.

"Perfect," Leo said, but in a way he was glad. They needed the fuse and the only way they were going to get it was to first find out who'd taken it. At least Remi followed Leo's instructions about Blop. There was only one sure way to make the robot go quiet: put him upside down in Remi's red jacket pocket. It was like putting him to sleep, something even Remi did once in a while for a break from the never-ending monotony of Blop's voice.

"If that's you, Jane Yancey, you're in big trouble!" Remi said once Blop was safely upside down in his pocket. "Loopa better not be up there! She could get loose in the elevator shaft!"

Leo thought Remi had said too much. What if it wasn't Jane Yancey? But he let it pass and gently knocked on the trapdoor.

"We know you're up there," Leo said. "You stole our fuse."

The door, Leo knew, snapped shut from the inside. A person could get trapped up there by accident if he or she didn't know the proper way to open it.

Leo looked at Remi with a look that said *Be ready to run*, and then he unlatched the trapdoor and pushed it up a few inches.

At first there was no one, just a long silence as Leo guided the door up another inch or two. Then four dirty knuckled fingers appeared over the edge of the door, pulling it all the way open.

"I don't think it's Jane Yancey," Remi whispered.

A second hand drifted out above the opening, holding the missing fuse.

"Looking for something?" a voice asked.

"Oh no," Leo said.

"What?" Remi responded, because he didn't recognize the voice, though he'd heard it in the basement once before from around a corner. "Who is it?"

"Why it's me, Mr. Carp, of course. Who were you expecting, that Rickenbacker character? He's too big to fit up here."

"Why are you hiding on top of my duck elevator?" Leo asked.

Mr. Carp's head appeared over the edge of the door. His glasses had slid down to the end of his nose, making him look older than he was.

"I told you already — I'm supposed to keep an eye on you, make sure you don't try to leave or do anything shifty. It's my job."

"And you stowed away up there while we were in the Puzzle Room?" Leo asked. He was trying to keep Mr. Carp busy while he thought of a plan.

"Yes, well, I didn't mean to get stuck up here. Only to do my job, you see."

"Yeah, we see what you mean," Leo said. "You're serious about your job."

"You'll find I'm impossible to shake," Mr. Carp said proudly. "Like a bad cold or a wad of gum on your shoe. It's a gift."

Leo thought Mr. Carp was more like a bumbling inspector than a serious force to be reckoned with, but Leo was also smart enough to know that looks could be deceiving.

"How did you get our fuse?" Leo asked. "You were trapped up there."

"Not at first; that unfortunate part came later," Mr. Carp said. He explained that he'd put a Popsicle stick in the trapdoor so it would stay open, and when they'd left the elevator, he opened it and reached down, taking the fuse. The only problem? He knocked the stick away when pulling up the fuse.

"Before I knew it," Mr. Carp said, "the trapdoor was shut and I was up here."

"Can we have our fuse back?" Leo asked. "We're not going to leave the hotel. Promise."

"What's behind the books?" Mr. Carp asked. His tone changed slightly, as if he were no longer bumbling along but instead had struck upon something important he could benefit from.

"Hot dogs," Remi said. "And popcorn. It's just silly stuff like that. You know Merganzer, always with the strange rooms."

"You take me for a fool," Mr. Carp said somberly. "I could tell important people about this, you know. I could tell Ms. Sparks, and she'd come right up here and look for herself. You don't want that to happen, do you, Leo Fillmore? Just tell me. What's in there?"

"I'll tell you if you give me the fuse," Leo said.

Mr. Carp seemed to consider the option, but he didn't answer right away.

"Nice mustache," Remi observed. He'd seen it from a distance in the basement and had wanted to say something about it. Remi dreamed of growing a thick mustache someday.

"It takes many years," Mr. Carp said proudly, "a mustache like this. You'll get there one day."

"You think so?"

"With a head of hair like that? I *know* so."

Sometimes Remi was smarter than Leo realized. Mr. Carp's only friend, as far as Leo could tell, was a stinky cat. Remi's compliment was a rare treat for a man like Mr. Carp.

"So a trade, then — the fuse for the information."

"Promise?" Mr. Carp asked. His intentions were impossible to read, but Leo nodded just the same. They were completely stuck without that fuse.

Mr. Carp tossed the fuse down and Leo caught it, carefully handing it to Remi with a wink. In the space of two seconds, Leo had the rainbow key card out of a pocket, sliding it along the corner of the duck elevator, sending the walls into a dancing display of colors as Mr. Carp looked on in wonder.

"That's quite a trick," he said, inching his way around the edge of the trapdoor for a better look. Leo secretly handed Remi the beaker key card, the one they'd gotten from Ingrid, just as the wall of the elevator slid away.

"What was that?" Mr. Carp asked, for he couldn't see the wall in question from his perch. "And what about the room behind the bookshelves? What's back there? You promised to tell!"

Remi was on his belly in a flash, pulling out the old fuse and inserting the new one.

"It's a room full of dominoes," Leo said. "Thousands of them, all set up to be knocked down."

"I do love dominoes," Mr. Carp said, smiling for an instant. "But why? What are they for?"

Remi looked up at Leo and Leo nodded.

"Better hold on to the cable, Mr. Carp," Leo said.

Mr. Carp looked as though he had a mind to scold the boys further until they spilled the beans about what was really hidden in the room, but he didn't get the chance. Suddenly, without warning, the duck elevator was moving.

Fast.

"I tried to warn yooooouuuuuuuuu!" Leo shouted. Remi had inserted the beaker card. He'd gotten out of the way just in time as the wall slid back into place. And the elevator had dropped like a piano out a window.

"Hold on, Mr. Carp!" Remi screamed. "Hold on!"

But the trapdoor slammed shut as the duck elevator plummeted past the lobby, the basement, the Jungle Room. They could hear him up there screaming, so at least he had held on to the cable and wasn't free-falling down the elevator shaft.

"I'm not sure we should have left him up there," Remi said.

"At least now we know where he is," Leo said as the duck elevator started to slow down. "And he can't get out."

"Actually, you're right!" Remi said. "Ha! This is perfect!"

As the elevator came to an abrupt stop, they heard Mr. Carp yelling for them to let him out. It was a muffled cry for help, but it sounded like he was unharmed.

"Don't worry, Mr. Carp!" Remi yelled at the ceiling. "Technically, we're still in the hotel. You're doing a great job!"

Leo and Remi smiled at each other. They even giggled a little bit. Everything was going to be just fine.

"Shall we open the elevator doors and see what Dr. Flart's dungeon looks like?" Leo whispered. He thought it best to keep Mr. Carp in the dark about where they really were, but Remi was too excited for that kind of nonsense.

"Flart's Fizz, here we come!" he yelled, opening the elevator door with a huge grin on his face.

There was a muffled call from above that sounded to Leo like "What's Fnarts Flizz?" He laughed, thinking of the tremendous adventure they were on.

But then the doors were open and he was looking into Dr. Flart's dungeon.

All the color ran out of his face. His jaw went slack.

"This might not be as much fun as we thought," he heard Remi say.

"I think you're right," Leo answered.

And then they walked out into the first dungeon either of them had ever been in.

CHAPTER 7

DR. FLART

Dungeons, as a general rule, are the kind of place people hear a lot about but rarely see. Hearing about them is a creepy kind of fun, like hearing about a sunken ship full of treasures and secrets. But no one wants to be on the ship when it's sinking, and in the same way, being inside an actual dungeon takes all the fun right out of it.

The boys ran back into the elevator.

"Leo," Remi said with a shaking voice, "can we skip this part and go back to the hotel? I don't feel so good."

"I'm with you. The only problem is we don't have a fuse. The one we used is blown."

"So we're not leaving here until we get another fuse, is that what you're telling me?" Remi's shoulders were pinned against the back wall of the duck elevator, as far away from the door as he could get.

"And we have to get the four Floogers. And the iron box. Remember?"

Something moved across the floor outside, casting a strange shadow into the elevator.

"What was that?" Remi whimpered.

Outside the elevator there was a room filled with all kinds of things that were loads of fun to read about but not very nice to be near. Remi's mind raced as his eyes darted between objects and terrors.

A table with chains and clasps for holding hands and ankles. *For stretching people!*

Walls of stone with ropes hanging from them. *For holding prisoners!*

Swords and maces and giant hammers. *For beating people up!*

Huge cobwebs made by king-size spiders. *For eating your face off!*

As Remi inventoried all the terrible things in the dungeon, he heard a series of sounds that didn't seem to belong next to one another. His mind was racing with possibilities.

A whimper. *Is that a rabid animal?*

A snort. *Yes! A rabid animal! Or a monster!*

The mechanical sound of hydraulics moving up and down. *A diabolical robot?*

The sound of steam pouring out of . . . something. *Yes! A diabolical robot! Or a death machine!*

"What is that?" Leo asked.

"If you get out of here alive and I don't," Remi said, pulling Blop out of his pocket, "take good care of Blop for me, will ya?"

"No, don't!" Leo said, but it was too late. Remi was hugging Blop like a stuffed animal.

"Did someone say my name?" Blop asked.

Leo tried to make Blop stay quiet, but it was impossible to keep the little robot from commenting on everything he saw. He started by asking Remi why he was sitting in the elevator acting like there was a monster outside. But then Blop's head swiveled around and he took a good look into the dungeon.

"Oh no," Blop said, his head spinning back and forth in short, rapid bursts. "Why did you come down here? Take me back! TAKE ME BACK!"

This had the appearance of a very bad omen. If Blop was freaking out, they'd definitely arrived in a place they shouldn't be.

Whatever had been making sounds where they couldn't see began to move again. It was coming closer, the shadow looming into the duck elevator like Ms. Sparks's beehive hairdo.

"We're all going to die!" Remi cried out.

"Unfortunately, that will not be happening," said Blop. "Please, Remi, put me back in your pocket before it's too late!"

The giant shadow covered the entire opening of the duck elevator. The awful sounds of slobber and steam and mechanical movements all clamored together, and Blop screamed. There is nothing quite as pitiful as a screaming five-inch-tall robot.

The monster of the dungeon had arrived in front of the duck elevator.

"What —?" Leo said.

Mr. Carp's muffled voice could be heard from above, asking if everything was all right. Remi had his eyes covered. Blop kept screaming in a tiny tin voice that was driving Leo insane. It was so bad, Leo got out of the elevator and stood in the creepy dungeon room next to the monster.

"Remi, open your eyes," Leo said. "It's fine. This thing's not going to hurt you."

Remi slowly moved his hand away from his face and opened his eyes just a little.

There was a thing that looked like a dog hopping up and down. It had four legs fashioned from brass pipes, coiled springs for feet, and steam chugging out of its metal ears.

"Wow, not what I expected," Remi said, and he began crawling out of the duck elevator.

"He can really bounce," Leo said.

The creature was very much like a dog, but it was made entirely of brass pipes and metal parts and wires.

"Calm down there, little buddy," Remi said. It wasn't that little. It was short and squat, in the shape of a plump bulldog. When Remi got close, the hopping stopped and the mechanical thing sat down, staring up at him with glassy eyes, steam shooting out if its nose in quick bursts.

Blop had gone cold and quiet, like he was trying desperately not to be noticed, but when Remi set him on the floor, he finally gave in.

"Hello, Clyde," Blop said. "Please stay calm."

Clyde and Blop clearly had some history. Clyde was fond of Blop. *Extremely* fond. She ran around in a circle, steam blowing out of every crack and crevice in her weird body.

"You *know* this thing?" asked Leo. "How?"

"I've been here before with Merganzer," Blop explained. "I'm afraid Clyde is a little bit over the moon for me."

"Clyde *likes* you?" Leo asked.

Before Blop could answer, he began to shake, like he was about to be magically pulled off the ground. Then, as fast as the eye could see, Blop shot across the floor and landed with a loud clang on Clyde's back.

"Blop!" Remi yelled. His robot had been kidnapped by a magnetically charged metal dog. He ran right up to Clyde and tried to pry Blop free, but it was no use. It was as if Blop were bolted to Clyde's back. The Franken-dog pranced around happily in a circle.

"What can I say?" Blop said. If he'd had robot shoulders, he would have shrugged them. "She likes the sound of my voice."

A burst of steam shot out of Clyde's upturned head, blasting Blop square in the face. Then Clyde began making beeping noises.

"She says she wants us to follow her," Blop translated.

"You're kidding," said Remi. "You can understand what she's saying?"

"Or course I can. I'm a robot."

Clyde bounced up and down, higher and higher, nearly touching Blop's head to the ceiling.

"I hate when she does this," Blop said.

"How are we going to get you back?" Remi asked.

"Oh, she'll get tired of carrying me around. Eventually. But for now, I'm afraid I'm stuck here."

Leo shrugged, not sure what else to do. At least Blop could understand Clyde. It was a start.

"Take us to your leader," Leo said, feeling much better about the dungeon as Clyde bounded mechanically toward the back of the spooky room. Everything felt less scary, more wacky, just the way Merganzer D. Whippet liked it.

Clyde stopped bouncing and started banging her head against the wall until Blop told Remi and Leo that it was a door they should open. It took them a few seconds to figure out all they had to do was push, and the wall drifted back on squeaking hinges. On the other side was a room less frightening than the one they were leaving.

Leo thought of Mr. Carp and felt guilty for leaving him behind. But what could he do?

"Hold tight, Mr. Carp!" Leo yelled behind him. "We'll be back before you know it!"

Clyde and Blop were already well ahead as Leo passed through the door into a high-ceilinged chamber.

"That's what I'm talking about!" Remi said, for this was less a dungeon and more the mad scientist's lab he'd hoped to find. "This is the stuff!"

A thick bolt of blue electricity streamed between two giant glass orbs hanging from springs on the ceiling; inside the glass, there was more electricity, moving in ghostly green and yellow patterns along the surface. There were tall round cylinders along the wall with dozens of rubber tubes sprouting out of their tops. Red and purple liquids ran through a hundred or more twisting clear tubes over their heads. A spinning belt wrapped over the top of a ten-foot flywheel turning in the center of the room. The wide belt disappeared into the floor, where the sound of pistons and gears leaked up through the concrete. There were platforms and ladders and piles of journals and drawings everywhere they looked. In the middle of the room, there was a square iron table, its sides covered in meters, dials, knobs, drawers, and buttons.

"I think I'm in love," Remi said, and Leo knew why.

The farthest wall back was made entirely of glass, and behind the glass sat row after row of Flart's Fizz. Remi began walking like a zombie toward the wall of bottles.

"Stay calm, Remi," Leo said, following close behind, taking in the surroundings. "We need to find Dr. Flart fast. There's no time for burping now."

Clyde bounced happily to her doghouse, which was in the corner and made of rivets and sheet metal. She tried to go through the door, but Blop banged into the frame and stopped her cold. Much beeping ensued as she tried again and again, each time with a little more force.

"She's not the smartest tool in the shed," Blop said, banging into Clyde's house before adding, "Takes her a little while to figure things out."

Leo didn't have time to feel bad for Blop, because Dr. Flart's mad scientist's lab suddenly filled with the sound of a tremendous burp, followed by an explosion and a burst of light in one of the tall cylinders against the wall. The door blew open, pouring smoke, and a man stumbled out.

"Clyde!" the man bellowed. "Bring me another!"

Clyde immediately stopped what she was doing and bounced on her springy feet toward the bank of dials and knobs and buttons along the table in the middle of the room. The man didn't seem to notice Remi and Leo standing in the shadows, and neither boy felt the urge to start talking. Clyde beeped and whirled. Steam shot out of her ears.

"I haven't got all day!" the man yelled. He had turned around and shoved his head back inside the cylinder, pulling out gobs of wires and adjusting things Leo and Remi couldn't see. Even hunched over, the man was very tall.

Clyde tapped her metal nose on a button and a claw attached to the ceiling by a coiled cord moved across the room. It plummeted to the floor near the glass wall, and when it reappeared, the claw was holding a bottle of Flart's Fizz.

"Which button did she push?" Remi whispered. Leo elbowed him in the shoulder as the bottle arrived in front of Clyde. The mechanical dog picked up the bottle between her wide metal jaws and carried it to the cylinder. Clyde beeped loudly and the man reached back his hand without turning around. A moment later he stood, banged his head on the edge of the cylinder door, and took a closer look at the bottle through the thickest pair of glasses Leo had ever seen.

"I specifically asked for grape, did I not?"

Clyde beeped and shook her head back and forth.

"No, no. I did, I said grape. I'm sure of it."

He leaned forward, setting the cap of the bottle between Clyde's metal teeth, as if he were about to use the Franken-dog as a bottle opener.

And that's when the man saw Blop.

"What do we have here?" Dr. Flart said curiously, squinting his eyes through his thick glasses. "Is that? No, no — it can't be."

"Hello, Dr. Flart. It's been a while," Blop said.

Dr. Flart looked confused, scratching the wild tuft of white hair on top of his head.

"So it has," he said at length. "So it has, indeed."

He popped the cap off the bottle of Flart's Fizz and Clyde's head spun in a circle, steam pouring out everywhere, beeping like a lunatic robot. Dr. Flart didn't pay any attention. Instead he guzzled every last drop from the bottle in one continuous monster glug. He got a funny look on his face, shook his head back and forth, and then let out the puniest of burps. It barely made a sound.

"Another dud," he said, setting the glass bottle on the metal table with a clang. "Two in one day. What are the odds?"

"I didn't come down here on purpose," Blop complained. He was in an irritable mood, probably because of all the body blows at Clyde's doghouse. "Those two idiots brought me."

"Two idiots, you say?" Dr. Flart swung his head around as he took in the whole of his laboratory.

"Over here," Leo said halfheartedly, stepping out of the shadows and pulling Remi along by his red jacket.

Dr. Flart weaved back and forth, ducking under a low beam as he moved cautiously toward Leo and Remi. He was thin and wiry, pushing seven feet tall, and he leaned down with his hands folded behind his back when he arrived within a foot of the boys.

"I'm a fan of your drink," Remi said.

"Wherever did you get one?" asked Dr. Flart. He didn't wait for an answer. "And what are you doing in my dungeon?"

"Merganzer sent us," Leo said before Remi could start asking for more bottles of Flart's Fizz. "And we got the drinks from Ingrid, upstairs."

"In the Jungle Room," Remi added.

Dr. Flart had gone a little soft in the face somewhere in the middle of all this, his eyes drooping and gigantic behind his glasses.

"Merganzer D. Whippet, the one and only," he said.

"Yes, that's the one," Leo said with a smile. "He asked us to gather some things for him, so that's what we're doing."

"Ingrid gave us the zip rope," Remi explained, nodding with pride.

Dr. Flart stood straight up and banging his head on one of the beams.

"You should move some of those things," Remi said. "You're going to hurt yourself."

"Keeps me alert, agile. But it's a thought."

Dr. Flart seemed to be seriously contemplating the idea of removing some of the lower beams as he looked around his work space.

"We were wondering," Leo said nervously, unsure if

he should ask, "you see, we're on a tight schedule, and there are some things we're looking for. . . ."

Dr. Flart held the watch on his wrist extremely close to his face, clapped his hands twice, and walked away. He shouted over his shoulder as his white lab coat trailed behind him.

"Come along, time to eat! We'll get this all straightened out over dinner."

Remi and Leo were famished . . . but they were also nervous about going too deep into the dungeon, away from the door that would lead them back out. Still, the idea that dinner might include Flart's Fizz and all kinds of other fantastical menu items was enough to get them both moving as Clyde went ahead, encouraging them along.

"You don't really think we're idiots, do you, Blop?" Remi asked as Clyde bounced up and down, hitting Blop's head on one of the beams as they went. Clyde didn't seem to notice.

"Don't answer that," Leo said, and they kept walking until they reached a corner that turned to the left. Inside sat a large table, and around the table, all kinds of strange containers bubbling and frothing with foam and goop.

But it was the walls that made Leo and Remi stop in their tracks. They were very high, thirty feet or more.

And the walls were something altogether more dun-geonlike: scary, creepy, weird.

All around them — the floor, the ceiling, the walls — was clear glass.

And behind the glass, tons and tons of dirt.

And in the dirt, many, many tunnels big enough for Leo to crawl through.

And in the tunnels, ants.

BIG ants.

Bigger than rats.

Bigger than Clyde.

Bigger than Remi!

CHAPTER 8

THE ANT FARM

I call this stuff Glooooob," Dr. Flart said. He had the handle of what appeared to be a gas station tire pump in his hand. There was a long clear tube behind him full of something green and gloppy-looking. The handle had a thumb depressor, and Dr. Flart pushed it, sending a bright green stream of Glooooob sailing through the air.

"I'm going in!" Remi yelled — his fear of giant, man-eating ants wasn't enough to keep him out of a room filling up with crazy green Glooooob. Clyde bounced up onto the table as Dr. Flart hosed her down with Glooooob, then he pointed the hose into his own mouth and glugged four or five mouthfuls.

He stopped spraying Gloooob and smacked his lips a few times.

"Sour," he said, "like Pixy Stix. I might have over-cooked it just a tad."

"Sour like Pixy Stix?" Remi said, and then Dr. Flart shot him in the face with the Gloooob and Remi had his first taste of something so delicious, he couldn't put words to it.

"Get in here, Leo! It's better than the Cake Room in the hotel!"

Leo reluctantly took two steps into the room, and Dr. Flart blasted his curly head of hair with Gloooob. Some of it ran down Leo's face and into his mouth, and that was all it took to get Leo into the action.

Gloooob was sour, sweet, syrupy, sparkling perfection.

And the best part? What didn't get eaten bubbled and fizzled and *poof!* It was gone.

"Dr. Flart, you're a genius!" Remi said.

"So I've been told. Try this one."

And so they went from tube to tube, showering one another and the room with every color of the rainbow. After a while they calmed down a little bit, sat in the chairs, and each held a different tube.

"Which one is this again?" Remi said, shooting Leo in the face.

"That's the Flooooob," Dr. Flart said. "The blue one is the Zooooob, blueberry bubble gum fizz, my personal favorite. I like to get my fruits at least once a day."

"How'd you make this stuff?" Leo asked. It was awfully tasty, and the way it vanished like Flart's Fizz made him like it even more. No cleanup.

"Simple molecular gastronomy, my boy. Nothing to it," said Dr. Flart, and then he shot Remi square in the chest with a bubbling stream of pink Flooooob.

"Cotton candy!" Remi howled. He was in heaven.

It was a lot of fun, but Leo had been watching the ants and thinking about Mr. Carp and Ms. Sparks and the hotel and the things he should have been getting. He was more of a worrier than Remi was.

"Dr. Flart, can I ask you now about the things we need?" Leo interrupted. "And about the ants? They're big."

Dr. Flart and Remi stopped laughing and carrying on.

"Don't worry about the ants — they can't get out. Unless I let them out."

Leo gulped. "But you're not going to do that, right? I mean, you don't have to walk them or feed them or anything? They stay in there?"

"That they do. They have a purpose, you see. But I'm guessing you already know that."

Merganzer hadn't said anything about giant ants or Glooooob or a lot of things. Remi shot Leo in the ear with Flooooob, then stuffed the tube down Leo's maintenance overalls and kept filling them up until his stomach stuck out like a giant balloon.

"Ha ha ha," Leo said, punching himself in the stomach and sending Flooooob into the air like giant globs of pink shaving cream. Seconds later, it was gone, fizzled away into thin air.

"What we need," Leo said, "are four Floogers and the iron box."

Dr. Flart had just taken a huge tap hit of Zooooob and he sprayed it in Leo's general direction.

"Four Floogers and the iron box?" he said, clearly upset. "Are you sure that's what Merganzer asked for? Not something else?"

Leo was starting to wonder about the Floogers and the box. Ingrid had reacted in pretty much the same way.

"That's what he said, I'm sure. Ask Remi, he'll tell you."

"It's true," Remi said. "And a six-pack of Flart's Fizz."

"Remi." Leo's eyes narrowed.

"Okay, I made that part up. He wants a case. No wait, *ten* cases!"

Leo rolled his eyes and Remi laughed.

"Four Floogers," Dr. Flart mused to himself. He stood up. "*And* the iron box? Something big is happening. Something huge."

"Why does everyone keep saying that?" Leo asked. "What's Merganzer got you doing down here?"

Dr. Flart shook his head as if he'd been dreaming and touched the wall of glass where a four-feet-long ant was crawling by.

"Merganzer D. Whippet is my benefactor. In other words, he pays for everything. He set this laboratory in motion."

There was a sadness in his voice, like something terrible was about to happen to his work.

"What's wrong, Dr. Flart?" Remi asked.

Clyde made a series of sad beeping sounds.

"It's just . . . well, I've been working for a long time. But it appears my work may have come to an end."

"No way!" Remi said. "You've got to make more gastromagical stuff! You can't stop now!"

"My dear boy, I'm afraid this is all just for fun, to pass the time. The real work has been done for months."

"The Floogers and the iron box?"

Dr. Flart nodded slowly, looking in at the ants once more.

"Tell us, Dr. Flart. What's a Flooger?" Leo asked.

"And what's the iron box for?" Remi added, his mood shifting as things turned more serious.

"It's a lot of power. And a place to put something very dangerous."

Leo thought about this for a moment. *A lot of power.* Ingrid had said that, too.

Dr. Flart started walking back and forth rapidly, his hands waving around as he talked to himself, working something out in his head.

"What's he doing?" Remi asked.

"Did he say how long?" Dr. Flart interrupted. "How much time do I have?"

"He didn't say exactly. But there's another problem, too."

Leo proceeded to tell Dr. Flart about the seven million dollars in back taxes, Ms. Sparks, all the bad news.

"That does complicate things," Dr. Flart said. "We can't lose the hotel — that would be a disaster. And there's only one place you can find that much money in a hurry."

"A bank?" Remi asked.

"Okay, there are two places."

"Fort Knox?" Remi asked.

"Okay, three — but seven million that belongs to Merganzer D. Whippet — that kind of money can only be found if you go deeper."

"Deeper," Leo said. "Like where the gears are?"

"Yes, where the gears are. Only one person can run the gears, and I haven't seen him in a very long time."

"Who? Merganzer?" Remi was bursting with curiosity.

"Don't worry about that now — we've got real work to do!"

And with that, Dr. Flart was down on his knees, tinkering with something near the floor.

"Clyde! Pronto!" he yelled.

Clyde leapt off the table in one bounce and landed at Dr. Flart's side.

"Screwdriver!" Dr. Flart yelled.

Three jets of steam shot out of Clyde's head and her right leg came up. Dr. Flart grabbed the leg, turned it, and yanked it off.

"That's gotta hurt," Remi said, but Clyde only beeped and whirled and steamed.

"She's fine," Blop said. "But you should know something."

"Crowbar!" Dr. Flart yelled. He stuck the leg back on Clyde, turned her in a circle, and yanked it back off again. The end was a Phillips screwdriver.

"Does this look like a crowbar to you?" Dr. Flart scolded Clyde. Clyde beeped in a way that sounded nervous. The leg went back on.

"Crowbar!"

"What should we know?" Leo asked Blop. Dr. Flart was acting more like a mad scientist with every passing second, and Leo remembered Ingrid's warning: *He's . . . unpredictable.*

"He's opening it up," Blop said.

"Opening what up?" Remi asked. Even he was starting to get nervous.

"The ant farm. He's definitely opening the ant farm."

Dr. Flart was leaning hard into Clyde's crowbar leg, which was wedged into a crack in the glass. He was putting all his weight into it.

"Are you sure that's a good idea, Dr. Flart?" Remi asked. "Maybe we should have a soda, think about this a little more, really weigh our options."

"Stand back!" Dr. Flart said.

A small square of glass popped free and dirt trickled out onto the floor. Dr. Flart put his head into the opening. Remi and Leo could hear his voice echoing inside the ant farm.

"Yooooohooooo. Anyone in there?"

A pile of dirt fell into his substantial head of white hair.

"He's lost his marbles," Blop said. "We're in big trouble."

"Nonsense," Dr. Flart said, pulling his head out and shaking the dirt free like a wet dog just out of the bathtub. "All is as it should be. I'll need a volunteer."

Dr. Flart put Clyde's leg back on and twisted it into place.

"No one?" he asked, standing at his full height and staring down at the boys.

Leo and Remi both backed up a few steps.

"Oh, come now," he said, reaching under the table to a compartment Remi and Leo couldn't see. "The ants aren't *that* big."

Leo tried to remember everything he'd ever learned about ants. He seemed to recall that they could lift twenty times their own body weight.

"How much do they weigh?" Leo asked, gulping as Dr. Flart opened the secret door under the table and dry ice steamed out.

"46.938 pounds," Blop said. "A rough estimate, mind you."

Leo tried to do the math. Forty-seven times twenty.

Almost a thousand pounds.

Dr. Flart pulled out three bottles of Flart's Fizz and set them on the table. He fished around in his pocket and pulled out golf tees, gum balls, and a bottle opener.

"There we are," he said. "You're all set."

Remi was mesmerized by the Flart's Fizz. He was head over heels for the stuff, and Dr. Flart could tell.

"It's decided then. Clyde will guide you through the

ant farm to retrieve the Floogers while I take Leo into the lab for some very important work."

"Wait," Remi said, looking at the faces all around him. "You mean *me?*"

"Did you know an ant the size of a human can run as fast as a racehorse?" Blop asked. He went on an ant-fact tirade that included way more information than Remi wanted to know.

"Not to worry, my boy!" Dr. Flart said, yelling over the top of Blop's voice. "They have a mortal fear of loud noises. All you have to do is guzzle one of these if you see one coming toward you and they'll run for cover."

Dr. Flart picked up the bottles and set them into Remi's red jacket pockets. He put the bottle opener, which was tied to a string, around Remi's neck, slapped him hard on the shoulder, and bid him good-bye.

"Off with you! Clyde will show you the way. Oh — and don't touch both ends of a Flooger at the same time."

"Why not?" Remi asked nervously.

"You'll act as a conductor if you do that."

Dr. Flart looked at Remi, who was staring back blankly, as if he didn't understand.

"There's enough juice in one Flooger to light all of New York City for several days. You don't want that kind of power going live between your fingers. Based on my calculations, you'd instantly turn to dust."

"And we don't want that," Leo said.

"No, not that. That would be bad," Remi mumbled. It was all too much for Remi to calculate — the ants, the Floogers, the Flart's Fizz. He was in a nearly speechless daze.

Not so for Dr. Flart, who was full of energy and chatter, like there was a big, complicated experiment about to be done and he was in charge of all the details. He pushed Leo along, out into the laboratory, and Remi was left alone with Clyde and Blop in the dining room.

"He's right, you know," Blop said. "Merganzer designed it that way. Giant ants hate loud noises. The Fizz will protect you, I'm sure of it."

Clyde was staring into the hole, making a mechanical barking sound.

"See there?" Blop said from his perch on Clyde's back. "No ants. They don't like loud noises, just like Dr. Flart said."

Remi looked up the sides of the high glass walls. There were ants in there, lots of them, moving in the vast system of tunnels that ran overhead, underfoot, in every space of the wall. But it was true, none of the ants was anywhere near Clyde. They'd all moved away at the puny sound of her barking. Remi imagined what they'd do if he blasted a monster burp in their direction.

"But I don't even know what a Flooger looks like or

where to find one," Remi complained. He was starting to think he could go into the ant farm without completely melting down, but there was still the simple fact that he hadn't a clue about what to do once he got in there.

Clyde began bursting steam and beeping instructions.

"She says she'll show you where to go," Blop said. "Just follow her lead."

This made Remi feel better. He wasn't going alone — Blop and Clyde would be with him. And he had three bottles of Flart's Fizz! Things were looking up.

"She needs you to go in first," Blop said.

Remi crouched low and got his first look inside the ant farm. The hole stopped short and turned in both directions, and Remi realized something he hadn't before: Just like a small ant farm he might put in his room, this one was narrow. It was only a few feet deep, which meant the tunnels he had seen behind the glass were all the tunnels there were.

"Which way?" Remi asked. "Left or right?"

"Left," Blop said, translating a short burst of beeps and steam-filled whistles.

Remi turned to the left and started crawling along the floor of the dirt tunnel. It was heading up at an angle of about ten o'clock on a watch. It was a long tunnel, about twenty feet, and there were no ants in sight.

"This isn't so bad," Remi said. He could look to his left and see through the clear glass into the big dining room, which comforted him until he saw Clyde bouncing up and down in the far corner.

"I thought you were coming in with me!" Remi yelled. He couldn't hear Blop's answer, and it appeared they couldn't hear him, either. It was much harder trying to crawl backward, but he managed it, arriving at the bottom again to find another unfortunate surprise.

"Hey!" Remi yelled, hitting his fists on the glass. Clyde had moved the glass door back in place and sealed it shut (she was a clever robot dog, with advanced skills in biting things, holding on to them, and moving them). He could hear Blop's voice, but only barely through the thick glass. Something about not wanting any of the ants to get out.

Remi heard a strange noise from the tunnel on the right, like something big and curious moving toward him.

"Left!" Blop yelled in his biggest robot voice, which could hardly be heard inside the ant farm. Remi crawled back up the left tunnel as fast as he could, outracing the awful sound of ants chasing him.

Clyde moved all the way to the far corner of the room and began bouncing higher and higher until Blop's head nearly hit the glass ceiling.

"How did I get myself into this?" Remi asked himself. The tunnel switched back in the other direction and Remi kept climbing, trying to reach the top corner where Clyde was leading him. Soon he had switched back again and found himself looking down twenty feet at the table in the dining room.

Clyde had moved over, bouncing off the table and up to a spot on the glass ceiling where a group of ants were gathered.

Crawling on the inside of the glass ceiling was one of the scariest things Remi had ever done. He could think of only one thing: that the glass would break under his weight and he would fall. And then there were the ants — at least one following him, and more in front, gathered in a wider section of tunnel in front of him.

"Flart, don't fail me now," he said, pulling out the first of three bottles and popping the cap off. He drank it down before it could begin fizzing into thin air. It tasted as amazing as he'd remembered it to be.

He dropped the empty bottle and braced himself for a colossal burp as the ant behind him moved very close and the ants in front of him began to take notice of his presence.

Unfortunately, it was a dud. Not even a regular burp, but a true runt that lasted under a second and made almost no noise at all.

The ants were moving in fast now, curious and angry at an intruder in their midst.

Remi fumbled with the second bottle, dropping the opener several times as his hands shook. He wished he could turn around and see how close the ant (or ants) was behind him, but he was too big for that. And the line of ants in front of him was closing in fast.

The second bottle of Flart's Fizz made up for the first and then some. It packed such a wallop, Remi couldn't even chug the entire thing before a burp the size of Texas welled up inside him and filled the tunnel with a resounding blast of Fizz-filled air. The glass walls shook, the dirt walls crumbled, and the ants ran for their lives.

"HA!" Remi yelled. "Take that, you scrawny ants!"

He had wisely stuck his thumb over the opening of the bottle, and holding it up, he saw that there was still a quarter of Flart's Fizz left inside. Remi continued on another ten feet until he was over the center of the room, where Clyde was bouncing up to meet him about once every five seconds. It was twice as wide there and tall enough to stand, but Remi heard ants heading toward him once again. There were tunnels leading off in six or seven different directions on the ceiling of glass, and it sounded like ants were approaching from them all.

Remi looked up and saw that the ceiling was low enough to reach. More importantly, he saw the Floogers.

"Time to gulp!" he said, feeling emboldened by the power of his burps. He chugged the rest of the second bottle, then spun in a circle, machine-gunning burps down all the tunnels, sending giant ants running away as fast as their legs would carry them.

Remi set the bottle down as Clyde bounced a little too hard and bonked Blop's head into the glass ceiling with a loud clang.

"I found them!" Remi yelled, although he was pretty sure Clyde and Blop couldn't hear him as they plummeted back down to the table below.

There were four sticks of light poking out of the ceiling. They looked like blue neon tubes pulsing with life, and Remi got the feeling that the ants were the ones that had somehow created and maintained them. He reached up and took hold of one between his finger and thumb. It was very warm, not quite hot, and it didn't want to be removed from the ceiling. Remi gripped it tighter and hung from the Flooger with all of his weight. It began to slide slowly out of the ceiling, like pressure was building behind it, and then it popped loudly and Remi fell to the glass floor.

"I got one!" he yelled. He remembered about not touching it on both ends at one time and held the clear tube carefully in his left hand. It was the length of a spoon, and zigzagged in the middle like a lightning bolt.

"Cool," he said, watching the blue electricity dancing back and forth.

The popping sound should have made the ants scatter, but it was the one loud noise they weren't afraid of. In fact, it sounded to Remi like more ants than ever were moving toward him. If he could have seen the ant farm from the outside, he would have been alarmed. All the ants in the colony were moving toward him, for he was right: The Floogers were their creations, and they didn't like the idea of someone trying to take them.

Remi reached up and grabbed two more Floogers, one in each hand, and pulled them out. *POP! POP!* He put them in his pocket with the first and took out his last bottle of Flart's Fizz, opening it with a burst of bubbles.

"Please don't be a dud," he said, taking one giant swig and plugging the top with his thumb. He burped mightily, stopping the ants in their tracks, and grabbed the last Flooger. *POP!*

The ants were on the move again, but so was Remi. Clyde was still bouncing, moving along the table and guiding Remi across the ceiling in a tunnel no ants had found. He came to the end and began the switchback descent along the wall, making it all the way to the floor. He could see the glass door, the way out, but the biggest of the ants was waiting for him there, snapping its jaws angrily. Ants were close behind, too, and Remi gulped down the rest of the Fizz, producing a final burp that sent all the ants, even the biggest one at the glass door, fleeing for their lives.

The door flew open, Remi dove out, and Blop and Clyde cheered.

"Well done, Remi," Blop said. "Very well done. We were worried there for a minute, but you did everything exactly right. Also, Clyde would like to know if you'd be able to help her put the glass door back on, as the ants are coming."

Remi beamed. He'd done the impossible and gotten one of the things Merganzer needed: the four Floogers. They glowed warmly in his pocket as he attached the glass door and sealed the ants inside.

"Where are Leo and Dr. Flart?" Remi asked. "I gotta tell them about this!"

"If my calculations are correct, they're just about ready to fire the Wyro."

"Fire the whatso?" Remi asked.

"Follow me, I'll show you," Blop said. "This you don't want to miss."

And so Remi left Dr. Flart's dining room, but not before picking up the Zooooob hose and blasting the ants behind the glass, then turning it on himself for one last taste.

CHAPTER 9

FIRING THE WYRO

P HIPPS!"

Ms. Sparks was in no mood to deal with guests. Very soon she would own the Whippet Hotel and the property it sat on, and as soon as she did, she'd rip the hotel down immediately. She'd build a tower to rival Donald Trump's, make the roof her private residence, and never deal with a guest again as long as she lived.

"I'm telling you, I heard a monkey," Theodore Bump complained. "It's hard enough cranking out a novel a week with all the noise around here. I will not stand for a monkey squealing outside my door!"

"And I'm telling you we don't have monkeys at the Whippet," said LillyAnn Pompadore, who was doubling up on maid service until Pilar returned. "Only ducks. Lots of ducks."

"Is it so much to ask for a fluffier pillow?" said Mrs. Yancey. She was also standing in the lobby, bothering Ms. Sparks. "And someone find my daughter. She's vanished."

"I'll get to the bottom of these mysteries, pronto," Captain Rickenbacker said, whipping his cape behind him as he went into stealth superhero mode in search of monkeys and missing children.

Ms. Sparks heaved a great sigh of displeasure and screamed Mr. Phipps's name again as he entered the lobby. He was filthy.

"Don't you dare!" Ms. Sparks said, holding her flat palm straight out in front of herself. "Wipe your feet first."

The old Ms. Sparks, the one who had run the Whippet with an iron fist before being removed from duty, was incapable of letting a muddy-booted gardener into the lobby.

Mr. Phipps did his best to navigate the demands of the guests from where he stood. He'd been trying to reach Leo's dad all day, but he and Pilar were on a cruise ship in international waters without a phone. And neither Pilar nor Clarence Fillmore had ever been ones to check e-mail. Truthfully, Mr. Phipps had felt some guilt over the idea of trying too hard to reach them. It was their honeymoon, after all. Unless the hotel was on fire or toppled by an earthquake, it didn't feel right to bother them.

When the lobby cleared, Mr. Yancey appeared out of the shadows, glancing at his watch furtively.

"How much longer?" he whispered, though no one was there besides Ms. Sparks.

"When the clock strikes midnight, I'll start the auction," she said. "You just make sure you're there to place your bid."

"Three hours, I'll be there," Mr. Yancey said.

"Then we disperse, quickly, as if nothing has happened. An hour later, the hotel is ours."

"Brilliant!" said Mr. Yancey, slipping out of the room as quietly as a mouse.

He had already made out the check to the great state of New York for the full amount of the taxes in question — a pittance compared to what the land alone was worth. He had made many phone calls and done many calculations. The land was worth ten times what he would have to pay. It was going to be the biggest deal of his life.

No one else knew of the auction — Ms. Sparks had made sure of it. Within hours, the hotel and the land would change hands.

Ms. Sparks and Mr. Yancey would be its new owners.

"Stand back!" Dr. Flart yelled. When Remi entered the room, Dr. Flart and Leo were wearing long yellow rain jackets and welding helmets with small glass windows they could see out of. "This is going to be loud!"

The metal table in the middle of the room looked like it was straight out of a Frankenstein movie. Wires and pipes and tubes of electricity dangled overhead. The Frankenstein table was frightening to look at, except for the items in the middle of the table. This was no mad scientist's monster about to be made.

There were three things strapped down on the flat metal surface: a loaf of moldy bread, a box of crayons, and one very fluffy gerbil.

The gerbil was pleasantly eating a chunk of orange cheese. One of its tiny legs was tied to a big metal ring with a length of thread.

"What are you going to do to that harmless creature?" Remi asked, wide-eyed.

"Don't worry! He's going to be fine!" Dr. Flart yelled. His voice was muffled and, Remi thought, a little bit crazy inside the welding helmet. "Put on a coat and a helmet! No time to squander! It's firing!"

Remi had no idea what was going on, but he knew it was a bad sign that Clyde had bounced out of the room, back into the dungeon. Dr. Flart threw a bright yellow coat and helmet at Remi, and Remi put them on as fast as he could. Somewhere in the middle of putting on the coat and strapping on the welding helmet, he remembered what he'd done.

"Hey! You guys! I got the four Floogers!"

"Excellent!" Dr. Flart yelled. "I never doubted you for a second. Did you seal the door?"

"We did," Remi said.

"Very good. Difficult creatures to corral once they get free. Like herding cats."

"Way to go, Remi," Leo said. He'd moved closer to his brother, patting him on the back.

"CLEAR!" Dr. Flart screamed, like he was about to use paddles on a dead person in an attempt to revive him. He threw a lever and the whole laboratory lit up with zapping electricity.

And wow, was it loud. Like the Fourth of July — bangs and explosions and whirls almost too much to bear. A hot wind whipped through the lab, sending scientific papers flying everywhere.

"What's happening, Dr. Flart?" Leo yelled.

"And how's that gerbil doing?" Remi wondered out loud.

"The gerbil is dandy! Nothing to worry about! CLEAR!" Dr. Flart screamed.

He grabbed the lever and forced it down to the off

position. There was one more tremendous burst of light and sound as air was sucked up and out of the room, practically pulling Leo and Remi off their feet.

"You're nuts, Dr. Flart!" Remi yelled.

But Dr. Flart didn't answer.

All went quiet in the space of a heartbeat. Papers danced to the floor as if they'd been dropped out of the sky.

"Don't move," Dr. Flart said. His muffled words reached Leo and Remi, who stood as still as they could. Something on the Frankenstein table was glowing with every color of the rainbow. It was round, the size of a baseball, and it seemed to be spinning in every direction at once.

The loaf of stale bread was gone, and so were the crayons.

"You see there," Dr. Flart said. He had calmed down and stopped yelling everything he was saying. He lifted the welding helmet off his face and let it rest on top of his head. "He's just fine, not a scratch on him."

Remi and Leo came closer, taking off their welding helmets, too. When they stood next to Dr. Flart, he held out his cupped hands, and there was the gerbil, wide-eyed and shaking. Most of its fluffy hair had been singed off, revealing a surprisingly small gerbil under- neath. There was some smoke coming off his tail.

"You burned all his hair off," Remi said. "Not cool."

"It will grow back," said Dr. Flart, setting the small creature on the floor and watching it scurry away.

"What is that thing?" Leo asked.

"That, my dear boy, is a one of a kind. A Wyro. It's self-powered."

"That's impossible," Leo said, moving a little closer.

"Not true, not for Merganzer D. Whippet. I knew it was possible, and he believed. It takes two, sometimes."

Dr. Flart quieted then, as if he might shed a tear. Words failed him.

"Can I pick it up?" Remi asked.

"No, you may not pick it up," Dr. Flart said, sniffing. "There's only one way to move a Wyro."

"The iron box," Leo said, for he was sure that's what Dr. Flart meant to say.

"You're a perceptive one," said Dr. Flart. "I can see why Merganzer chose you."

Leo beamed at the praise, but he also worried over his hotel. Time was short — how short he couldn't know for sure — and he had yet to complete every task required of him.

"Come closer, if you want," Dr. Flart said. "Once I put the Wyro away, you won't be able to see it again until Merganzer uses it."

"Uses it for what?" Remi asked.

"That, my dear boy, is the billion-dollar question. I suppose only Merganzer knows what the Wyro is for."

Dr. Flart opened a drawer on the Frankenstein table and took something out: a square box, just big enough to hold a baseball. Leo could tell it was heavy by the way Flart picked it up. He turned the top, unscrewing the lid.

All three of them gathered around the table and gazed at the Wyro.

"Beautiful, isn't it?" Dr. Flart said wistfully. "So much power — even more than the four Floogers put together."

"My life just gets weirder and weirder," Remi said, his face at the same level as the Wyro as he watched it dance. It was as if there were a thousand concentric circles inside, all spinning in different directions, all different colors.

Dr. Flart carefully held the iron box upside down over the top of the Wyro, then he slammed it down, dragging it across the table. When he reached the very edge, he held the cover of the iron box just so, trapping the Wyro inside and, with some effort, turning the lid several times.

"Fetch me that duct tape, will you?" Dr. Flart asked Remi, lifting his chin in the direction of a shelf. Remi did as he was told, and shortly thereafter Dr. Flart had wrapped the iron box in several layers of silver duct tape.

"Amazing stuff," he said. "I wish I'd invented it. Or Post-it Notes. That was a biggie."

He held the iron box wrapped in silver tape out to Leo. Leo was nervous to take it, but besides the money, it was the last thing on Merganzer's list. He reached out and let Dr. Flart hand it over.

"But it's not possible," Leo said, smiling from ear to ear at the weight of the iron box. It was light as a feather.

"You two keep saying that," Dr. Flart said dreamily. "One day, you'll believe: Everything is possible. Only the limit of your imagination can stop you."

The iron box should have weighed at least ten or fifteen pounds, but Leo felt that he could let it go and it would almost float on the air like a balloon. It was practically weightless. The Wyro hummed quietly inside, and the iron box felt warm.

"It's out of my hands now," Dr. Flart said. He walked excitedly across the room, picked up a cheap plastic box used for holding index cards, and popped it open. There were at least a hundred cards in there. As Dr. Flart pulled out the front card, Remi saw that it was covered in small handwriting and diagrams.

"Oh, this *does* look interesting," Dr. Flart said. "I've got my work cut out for me."

Dr. Flart put the plastic box away, but he kept the card. He was completely overcome with his new assignment as Remi and Leo took off their yellow coats and welding helmets. They felt a sense of awe at Dr. Flart's single-mindedness. It was as if they no longer existed.

"Good-bye, Dr. Flart," Leo said as they came to the door of the dungeon that would lead them out. He stopped what he was doing, turned to them, and waved. He didn't speak, only looked at them in a way that made them sad and happy at the same time. He was so very excited to work on something new, but he was alone, or so it seemed until Clyde came bouncing back into the laboratory.

"Clyde!" Dr. Flart said. "I'm going to need at least three hundred brass tacks. And some of those corn nuts. And a hammer!"

Clyde bounded through the laboratory as Leo and Remi slipped through the door. Blop was waiting for them on the other side.

"The next time you decide to come down here," he said, "will you do me a favor and forget to bring me along? My head is killing me."

"But wasn't it exciting?" Remi said. "The ants and the Flooooob and — just all of it. I hope we *do* come back. And soon."

"There's something you should know," Blop continued as he rolled toward the duck elevator, which stood open.

"Don't tell me," Leo said. "You're going to miss Clyde after all?"

Blop rolled into the duck elevator and turned to face Leo and Remi.

"Mr. Carp has vanished."

CHAPTER 10

THE DOOR OF WARNINGS

Leo had a lot of pockets in his maintenance overalls. They came in many sizes and shapes for holding things like nails, bolts, air conditioner parts, plumbing wrenches, elbow pipes, doorknobs, and faucet plugs. There was one pocket in particular, large and empty, low on one leg, that was perfect for the iron box. It fit like a glove.

"Just make sure it doesn't fall out," Remi said, tapping the pockets on his red doorman's jacket. "The nice thing about these is the flaps. They hold everything in, like Floogers."

"We've got bigger problems right now," Leo said. They'd opened the trapdoor in the duck elevator and

Leo was peering into the open shaft above. "Blop was right. He's gone."

"How did you know he wasn't there before we opened the door?" Remi asked. Blop was in one of his pockets, where he liked it best.

"I yelled for him and he didn't answer. Either he was asleep or he was gone. I deduced he was gone based on the lack of space up there. According to my calculations . . ."

Blop went on and on about sleeping standing up, sleeping sitting down, and the decibel level of his own tinny voice, but Leo and Remi didn't pay any attention. They were busy climbing out of the duck elevator to have a look at where Mr. Carp could have gone.

"He'd have to be a monkey to climb out through the shaft," Leo said, which got Remi worrying about Loopa. "Don't start," Leo added before Remi could start in about the monkey. "You shouldn't have borrowed Loopa to begin with. I'm sure she's safe and sound in the Flying Farm Room."

He pulled Remi up through the opening and they both stood in the small space while Remi complained about Jane Yancey, the worst monkey babysitter on the planet.

The cable for the duck elevator went straight up into darkness. There were wooden plank walls on four sides, like a mine shaft, and Leo began banging on them one by one. When he got to the fourth wall, it sounded hollow, like there was nothing behind it.

"Can you turn Blop upside down?" Leo whispered.

Blop was right in the middle of a long-winded stretch having to do with how the brain operates when it's sleeping. Without waiting for the sentence to finish, Remi turned the little robot upside down in his pocket.

"That is one talkative robot," Leo said. "I don't know how you can stand it sometimes."

"You've obviously never been a doorman at the Whippet. It's insanely boring. I learn all sorts of great stuff from Blop."

"Shhhhh," Leo said. "We need to be quiet. There could be anything behind this wall."

Leo gently pushed on the wall of wooden planks. It didn't require much effort, and the wall swung in. The squeak echoed down a long, dirt-walled corridor behind the door.

"Cool," Remi said, peering in over Leo's shoulder.

The way down was lit by yellow lightbulbs dangling from the ceiling, each one leaving a drop of pale light on the brown surface below.

"Maybe we should go back up first," Leo whispered. "I mean, we have everything Merganzer asked for."

"Everything but the money," Remi corrected.

"But he didn't ask for that — Ms. Sparks did. I don't think he even *knows* about that."

Remi shrugged. He didn't know what they should do.

"If Mr. Carp is down here, we should find him. He could be in trouble."

"Yeah, it's true. I feel bad we left him here all alone. If there's danger down there, he doesn't stand a chance."

Mr. Carp certainly had struck them both as a witless wonder. Sure, he could track Leo and Remi, but other than that, Mr. Carp seemed far more suited to pushing papers across a desk in a cubicle than going on an underground adventure where hazards lurked around every corner.

"Okay," Leo said, touching his maintenance overalls where he'd placed the iron box. "Just be careful not to lose a Flooger, and I'll be careful, too."

"You first, I'll follow," Remi said. Leo looked at him sideways. "You know," Remi added. "In case someone comes up behind us and tries to hit us with a baseball bat. I've got your back, bro."

Leo wasn't buying it, but at least he'd talked Remi into going with him. They stepped off of the duck elevator onto cold, packed dirt. The way down was steeper than it had looked, the angle pulling them both against their will. It was like running down a mountain trail: walking, then jogging, then realizing it won't be easy to slow down with the dirt crumbling underfoot and the path getting steeper and steeper.

"Whoa!" Leo yelled, trying to stop short. He'd been moving way too fast with Remi far too close behind, and suddenly the way down changed from a sloping path to a long flight of stairs. Leo stopped in time, but Remi didn't, bashing into him from behind and sending them both tumbling head over heels. When they landed at the bottom, bruised but unbroken, they started yelling:

"Check the Floogers!"

"Where's the iron box?"

"Blop? Blop, are you okay?"

They stood up, dazed and worried, and found the iron box lodged in a corner. Blop was still asleep, purring softly, so Remi didn't wake him. And the Floogers were unbroken.

"It's a small miracle everything is still okay," Remi said. "Close call."

"Thanks for having my back. That was spectacular," Leo complained.

"You stopped without warning me!" Remi protested. "It wasn't *my* fault."

Both boys kicked the dirt, standing as far away from each other as they could in the landing space. The stairs continued down, but neither of them was ready to keep going yet. They hadn't had a good fight since officially becoming brothers, so maybe they were due. And the situation was becoming more dire by the second, so tensions were running high. Leo, in particular, was starting to feel the pressure.

"I wonder what Ms. Sparks is doing to my hotel," he asked, staring at the wall. "I wish she'd just leave us alone."

Remi could hear the anxiety in his brother's voice, and it worried him. He knew one thing for sure: If Leo fell apart, the hotel was in real trouble.

"Listen to me, Leo," Remi said. He took Leo by the shoulder and spun him around, staring right into his eyes. "The Whippet is your hotel, not hers. She hasn't got a chance against us. Think about it. We've been through jungles and dungeons and we've burped our brains out for the hotel. We love the hotel! She can't win."

"And we've battled giant ants," Leo said, feeling a little better.

"And shot each other with Zooooob!"

"And borrowed a monkey tail!" Leo said.

"Actually, I don't think we're giving that back, but still, you're right. We got a super-elastic monkey tail!"

"Come on, Remi," Leo said. "Let's find Mr. Carp and get back up there. This is our hotel, and we're *not* letting Ms. Sparks get her hands on it."

"*Our* hotel?" Remi said. He was astonished. It had never, ever occurred to him that Leo might see things that way. Remi was just happy to have a job and a place to sleep.

Leo grabbed Remi by the shoulder. "Yeah, our hotel. And we're going to save it together."

Remi beamed, looked down the flight of stairs, and took the lead the rest of the way down.

"Don't follow to close," he called back. "I might stop short. And if someone comes up behind you —"

"I'll have your back," Leo said, finishing Remi's sentence for him.

The way down started to have fewer lightbulbs the farther they went. First there had been one every ten feet, then every twenty. But as they approached a landing and a turn, they peered around and saw only one dim bulb, way off in the distance, at least fifty feet away. Everything in between was pitch-dark.

"This is bad," Remi said.

"Mr. Carp?" Leo called. Then louder, "Are you there, Mr. Carp?"

There was no answer. Staring out into the blackness, Leo had to agree with Remi.

"You're right," he told his brother. "This *is* bad."

The one lightbulb looked like a single, faraway star in an otherwise black sky. They couldn't see the floor out there, and for all they knew, it fell away into a thousand-foot shaft they couldn't see.

"Hang on," Remi said, pulling out one of the four Floogers and holding it out in front of him. It radiated a faint blue light, electricity flowing back and forth under the glass, but it only showed them an extra few feet. He pulled the others out, holding all four together, but still, the darkness swallowed up most of what the Floogers had to offer in the way of light.

"I have an idea," Leo said. He took the iron box out of his maintenance overalls and started unwrapping it.

"I'm not sure Dr. Flart would approve," Remi said. "That thing is radioactive."

But Leo kept at it, pulling duct tape away like he was peeling a banana. He was careful not to remove the lid as he came to the last of the tape, letting it hang loosely along the sides of the iron box.

"Ready?" Leo asked.

"Not really."

Leo held the edge of the box, slowly turning the lid. Light burst forth, filling the space between where they stood and the faraway bulb. The Wyro began to shake and the iron box started getting heavier.

"It's clear, just a path!" Remi said, but Leo wasn't listening. The iron box had suddenly gotten so heavy, he couldn't hold it up any longer. He fell to the ground, the iron box pinning his hand to the dirt.

"Leo!" Remi yelled. "Close it!"

"I'm trying! It wants to come out!"

Leo was pushing down on the lid, which was also pushing down on his pinned hand, but the lid wasn't budging. There was still a crack where brilliant light burst out.

"I got this!" Remi screamed, putting his foot on the lid. His foot was also on Leo's hand. Between Remi's full weight and the weight of the iron box, Leo's pinned fingers were screaming with pain. It felt a lot like the time he'd gotten his fingers closed in a car door, but he didn't cry out. He kept his cool as the iron box closed shut and the light vanished.

"Okay, don't get off yet," Leo said through clinched teeth. "Let me slide my hand out from under your foot."

Remi was balancing with one hand against the wall. His other hand was busy putting the four Floogers back in his red jacket pocket. Leo slowly worked his fingers out from between Remi's doorman shoe and the iron box, then held the loose duct tape at the ready. Remi spun in a circle like a ballerina as he stood on the iron box, screwing it into place.

Leo's other hand was still pinned between the iron box and the ground, and Remi was still standing on the iron box.

"On the count of three, jump, then land again," Leo instructed. "Can you do that?"

"I can do it, but it's going to hurt."

Leo just shook his head. It was the only way. The Wyro was capable of unscrewing the lid if they didn't secure it with tape.

"One, two, three!"

Remi jumped, Leo wrapped one strip of silver duct tape over the lid, and Remi landed back on the iron box.

"Okay, that hurt a little bit," Leo said. "One more time and we should have it secured for sure."

"Are you sure you can do this?" Remi asked. He felt awful having to jump up and down on Leo's hand.

"One, two, three!" Leo said without answering, and Remi jumped. Leo wrapped another thick strip of duct tape over the iron box, then told Remi to get off his hand.

The box was weightless once more, but Leo didn't move his injured hand until he and Remi had completely wrapped the box up again.

"You okay?" Remi asked, holding the featherlight box as Leo squeezed his fingers in and out of a fist.

"Nothing's broken, but wow, that hurt. I think I'm going to have some bruises."

"Better put this away," Remi said. "That Wyro is serious business."

"Thank goodness for duct tape."

Both boys looked out in the direction of the soft yellow light and started walking. It was a long way, farther than it had looked, and at the end, under the bulb, there was a door with a message stenciled in black paint:

WHIPPET PROPERTY.
DO NOT ENTER.
DANGER.
TURN AROUND.
GO AWAY.
DON'T COME BACK.
BOO!
WHY ARE YOU STILL STANDING THERE?

"He's a funny guy, Merganzer," Remi said.

"Mr. Carp has to be down here," Leo said, touching the doorknob, which matched the ones in the hotel upstairs. "Where else could he be?"

"It's kind of a lot of warnings, though, right? Is that normal for Mr. Whippet?"

Leo wasn't sure. It *was* a lot of warnings, but it was now or never.

Leo turned the handle and pushed the door open. He stepped through with Remi close behind.

What lay behind the door of warnings took Leo's breath away.

· CHAPTER 11 ·

INTO THE REALM OF GEARS

Whose cat is this?" asked Mr. Phipps. He was holding Claudius at arm's length, plugging his nose. "It's stinking up the basement."

He'd been trying to find Leo and Remi for over an hour with no luck. Checking the basement, he'd found Claudius sleeping on Leo's bed.

"Keep that thing away from me," said Ms. Sparks. "It belongs to Mr. Carp, and he's obviously done a poor job taking care of it."

"Well, then, where is this Mr. Carp? Did you bring him here?" asked Mr. Phipps. He was rather proud of himself for standing up to Ms. Sparks so forcefully.

Ms. Sparks hadn't seen Mr. Carp for hours, and it

was unnerving her as well. The little doofus only had one task — keep an eye on those kids! And this, suddenly, bothered her, too. She looked outside through the main doors of the lobby, where night had settled in, and wondered, *Where are Leo and Remi? What are they up to?* She'd been so focused on the clock — only two more hours to go! — she'd forgotten all about them.

"Where are those boys, Mr. Phipps?"

"You're not really helping about the cat," Mr. Phipps replied. "So I'll assume you want me to put it outside."

He dropped Claudius, and the cat turned on Mr. Phipps, hissing at his leg. It walked, very slowly, toward Ms. Sparks. Ms. Sparks stood stock-still, staring down at the smelly cat, until it purred against her leg, leaving a trail of cat hair on her polyester slacks.

"Claudius," Ms. Sparks said, for she had liked the way the cat had hissed at Mr. Phipps. "Go outside and kill mice. Make yourself useful."

The cat couldn't have understood, but he had been interested in the garden and the pond ever since setting eyes on it. He was all too happy to be shooed out the door.

Ms. Sparks looked at her watch, then glared at Mr. Phipps.

"I demand that you keep this lobby clear of anyone but Mr. Yancey. I will not stand for that lunatic

Rickenbacker or pompous Mr. Bump! Keep them away from me, understood?"

Mr. Phipps didn't understand why the guests of the hotel couldn't move about the hotel they were paying to stay in, but he nodded just the same.

Something was up; he only wished he knew what it was.

When the lobby was clear, Ms. Sparks took out the special papers she'd been given the authority to fill out. She'd already carefully filled in every piece of information. By law, people had been invited to the auction. She'd sent out all the invitations to every known developer worth their salt in the entire state. Too bad for them those letters had all been accidentally mailed to a PO box owned by Ms. Sparks.

In one hour and fifty-seven minutes, the auction would take place on the steps of the Whippet Hotel. Only one bidder would arrive with his sealed offer, just enough to cover the taxes and a promise to make the property produce much more tax revenue in the future. Exactly what the governor wanted. Even Merganzer D. Whippet, with his vast resources, couldn't offer the great state of New York a skyscraper producing tens of millions in income for the city. Ms. Sparks knew what would make officials happy, and she could deliver it:

A clean transfer of title.

A moneymaking high-rise monstrosity on the property.

Tax revenue to die for.

Ms. Sparks could hardly contain her excitement.

But where were those boys? And Mr. Carp. Where was he?

—————

The ceiling was high, covered with fluorescent tubes of light hanging from long chains. The room itself was vast, as wide as a football field and just as long.

"I can see the reason for the warnings on the door," Remi said, stumbling a few feet forward as he gazed into the open room.

It was cold like frozen metal, and both boys could see their own breath. Giant circular gears as tall as a house were intricately pieced together like the inside of a gigantic watch. Steel beams ran all through the room, connecting gear to gear to gear. This thing was a monster, a colossus.

"I don't even know what to say," Leo said. "This time, Merganzer has completely outdone himself. What on earth could this be for? And how could he have built it?"

Nothing moved, which made the Realm of Gears a scary place. There was something about the stillness of such huge, dangerous objects connected to one another that left a ghostly dread in the air.

"It hasn't been turned on in a while," Remi said. "At least it doesn't seem like it."

"My hunch is you're right, but what's that noise?" Leo was listening intently, trying to get a better feel for a sound from far away. "It's coming from over there. Come on."

Leo moved cautiously in the direction of the sound, carefully stepping around and under the gears. It was like walking through the inside of a great grandfather clock that had stopped ticking. Everything was hard-edged, cold, mechanical.

"Should I wake Blop up?" Remi asked. "He might know about this place."

"I don't think we should. Let's just see what the sound is. We're almost there."

They passed between three gears that were so close together, there was only room for them to slide through sideways.

"I feel like it's alive," Remi said, watching his cold breath as his breathing became choppy and afraid. "Like it's going to wake up and tear us apart."

Leo didn't answer right away. He felt the same way, but he knew it wouldn't help the situation if Remi knew they were both terrified. Leo was also afraid for a different reason. He'd never been this far underground, and it felt desolate in a way he'd never felt before.

He tried to put on a brave face. "It's going to be fine. Just keep moving, and don't think too much."

The sound was getting much louder, and both boys thought they knew what it was as they came to the opening of a tunnel leading down farther still.

"It's gears, don't you think?" Remi asked.

Leo nodded, and as they crept slowly into the tunnel, they saw that it was true. There were smaller gears, the size of a tractor tire, spinning inside. Half of each gear was underground where they couldn't see, but they were definitely spinning.

"Why are these gears moving?" Leo asked out loud, though he was really asking himself.

Curiosity got the better of them and they crept farther inside, each of them standing on the opposite side of the gears, which ran down the middle of the tunnel.

"They're getting smaller," Leo said. "That's weird, right?"

"Kind of, yeah," Remi said. "And the ceiling is getting lower. *Everything* is getting smaller."

Twenty feet later, they were both crouched down low, the gears the size of dinner plates grinding against one another. Up ahead, the tunnel curved to the right, to places they couldn't see.

"Um, Leo?" Remi said.

"Yeah?"

"These aren't gears."

"What do you mean they're not gears? Of course they are."

Leo's eyes had been adjusting to the light, and he hadn't been watching as closely as Remi had. When he took a closer look, he saw that Remi was right. The spinning had slowed, and the teeth of the gears were sharp.

"They're saw blades, not gears," Remi said. "That can't be good, right?"

Leo was starting to feel afraid. "Let's just get to the curve and see what's on the other side. That's as far as we'll go."

Remi moved ahead, crawling as he went, sensing a sparkling sort of light around the corner. The gears were sharp as dragons' teeth, but at least they had gotten even smaller, like dozens of spinning saucers.

"Sharper, but smaller," Leo said. "Why?"

They rounded the corner and found that it opened into a dazzling cave of glittering light. They had discovered one of the best-kept secrets in the world, and the true source of Merganzer D. Whippet's vast fortune.

The Whippet diamond mine.

"That's it, I'm waking Blop," Remi whispered. "He's gotta see this."

"No, don't. He'll only distract us," Leo whispered back, putting his hand on Remi's arm. It was a dangerous thing to do, because the blades were spinning right underneath his elbow.

"Let's get a closer look. Take it slow," Leo cautioned. Remi nodded and the two boys crawled carefully into the open space of the diamond mine. It was ten or eleven feet high and just as wide, with diamonds shimmering like stars from the floor to the ceiling.

"If Mr. Yancey or Ms. Sparks finds out about this, it could be real trouble," Leo said.

"And Mr. Carp is down here somewhere," Remi added. "That can't be good."

They both spun in a circle and couldn't help but smile. The room represented so much money, they couldn't wrap their young brains around it.

"There must be a hundred million worth, you think?" Leo laughed.

"A hundred *billion*," Remi said, but it was anyone's guess.

Leo moved in close to one of the craggy walls and found small spinning blades whirling quietly. They appeared in the stone at various places, some as small as a quarter, whirling around silently.

"I bet they're for cutting away the stone or something like that," Leo said, amazed at how peculiar it all was. The cave made a T at the end, heading off in two directions. Turning one way led to what appeared to be more and more diamond and blade–encrusted walls of stone. To the left was a different story.

"Is that . . . ?" Remi started to ask, then paused and tilted his head to the left as he sometimes did when he was trying to sort out a puzzling situation. "A pink rhinoceros?"

Leo knew the wacky logic of a pink rhino head blasting out of a cave without having to think twice about it. He didn't waste any time walking up for a closer look.

"It's like Daisy, the shark in the Whippet basement. Only this one's a rhino."

"And it's pink, which isn't making it look any less like it wants to skewer me with its horn."

The horn was bright white, the face poised to strike, with an angry snarl that seemed, somehow, hilarious.

"Its name is Petunia," Leo said, reading the brass nameplate beneath the snarl. "How dangerous could she really be?"

There were other things in the corner of the diamond mine as well, and Leo and Remi sorted through them, beginning to understand:

- *A clear plastic tube for putting things in, like the ones at a bank drive-through that get sucked*

into a long pipe and end up in the hands of a
teller.
- Two holes in the cave wall, one marked OUT, one
marked IN. There was a button over the one
marked OUT.
- A table under Petunia's head with a scale,
weights, charts, notepads, pencils, and bowls of
cut diamonds.
- And lastly, a big pink button, the size of Remi's
head, on the floor under the table, which Remi
accidentally stepped on while freaking out over
the incredible pile of cut diamonds.

Stepping on the giant pink button made smoke bil-
low out of Petunia's nose. She made a sound like she
might come barreling the rest of the way out of the
wall, and then was silent.

A pink strip of ticker tape printed out of Petunia's
mouth. Leo pulled it off.

"Just like Daisy," he said.

"Merganzer is the coolest." Remi smiled, running
his soft fingers over the bowl of diamonds. "What's
it say?"

Leo read the instructions: "'NY Taxes, present day
calculation: $7,121,321.46. Property default in sixty-five
minutes.'"

"Wow, that interest rate is harsh," Remi said. "Remind me never to get a credit card."

"And we've only got an hour. How could Merganzer let this happen?"

Remi picked up the bowl of shiny diamonds and poured them into the container that sat on the scale. Then Leo started setting weights on the other side. When the scale was exactly even, he saw that there were four pounds of diamonds on the scale.

"That's a lot, right?" Remi asked.

"I think it depends on the quality," Leo answered, picking up the chart sitting on the table. There were all kinds of drawings and notations someone had made.

"That looks complicated," Remi said.

Leo read some of the categories that made diamonds valuable: "Shape, cut, color, clarity, karat."

It was impossible to know how much they had in front of them, except for the marking on the bowl the diamonds had been in.

"A-plus-plus-plus," Remi said, touching the rim of the bowl. "The best grade I've ever gotten was a B-minus, and I'm amazing. These diamonds must be perfect!"

"You might be right," Leo said. "But let's wake up Blop, just to be sure."

Remi thought that was a fantastic idea. He pulled Blop out and set him on the diamond table, where the little robot's eyes fluttered open.

"What was I saying?" Blop asked with his tiny tin voice. "Oh yes, about the . . ."

Blop's head moved from side to side, taking in the surroundings. Before he could speak, Leo grabbed him and pointed him in the direction of the pile of diamonds on the scale.

"These are grade A-plus-plus-plus diamonds," Leo said. "There are four pounds of them. How much is that worth?"

Sometimes, when Blop had a particularly difficult problem to solve, he would make small humming and beeping noises. When this happened, it could take a while to get him back.

"We don't have time for this," Leo said. He'd already put two and two together: The diamonds went in the tube in the hole marked OUT. What happened after that, he had no idea, but it had a certain wacky Whippet logic he had come to believe in.

Leo held the clear tube and Remi poured the diamonds in. Hearing them tumble against one another sounded like broken glass rolling around and around inside a barrel. Remi sealed the tube shut and turned it around in his hand. Beams of light danced off the cave walls, and Leo had a thought.

"Someone had to get all these diamonds cleaned up and made into A-plus-plus-plus."

Remi shrugged like he didn't really care, placing the end of the tube into the hole.

"It would be a lot of work, getting this many diamonds ready," Leo went on.

Remi wasn't paying attention. He was trying to figure out how to make the tube get sucked into the hole. The only button he could find was the giant pink one under Petunia's nose.

"You'd have to dig them out of the rocks, use all these different blades and tools to carve them just right. It would take some time, you know?"

Remi tapped his foot on the giant pink button again, just to see what would happen, and the tube was gone with the sucking sound of air.

"Do you think that was a good idea?" Leo asked. "We just sent four pounds of grade A-plus-plus-plus diamonds into an air hole."

Remi hadn't thought of that. The hole did say OUT, but that was all he'd really known. He felt a little dumb as they stood in the diamond mine without any cut diamonds, wondering what to do next.

Several minutes went by in silence as both boys waited and Blop calculated, then Petunia blasted some smoke out of her wide nostrils and pink ticker tape poured out of her mouth. Leo ripped it free.

"What's it say?" Remi asked, worried it was terrible news like *We are pirates — thank you for the four pounds of diamonds! Make more or we bring out the cannon!*

Leo read the pink ticker tape: "Word for word, it says: 'Assuming A-plus-plus-plus per usual. Comptroller reviewing account now. Where have you been hiding? The Gov.'"

"The *Gov?*" Remi couldn't believe the real governor of New York was sitting in a room somewhere with the diamonds. "Incredible!"

"I wonder how long it will take," Leo said. They still hadn't found Mr. Carp — he could be anywhere in the enormous room of gears — and the clock was ticking. By now it was late at night, pushing close to the midnight hour, when the Whippet might not be his anymore.

"Come on, Governor!" Leo yelled. "Get a move on!"

Blop whirled and beeped softly, calculating what Leo and Remi hoped would be a big number. His eyes fluttered again, as if he might go to sleep, but then he started to speak.

"Hold on!" Remi said, cutting Blop off before he could say anything.

Remi had heard something.

Something important.

The sound of air moving fast through a pipe.

"I think it's coming back!" Remi shouted. He got his face right up next to the hole marked IN and peered as if it were a spyglass.

"I don't know if I'd stand that close, just in case," Leo said.

The tube arrived with Remi's head in the way, which sent Remi flying backward, landing inches away from a whirling saw blade the size of a bottle cap.

"I'm okay!" Remi yelled before anyone could ask, hopping to his feet and rejoining his brother and his robot under Petunia's watchful gaze.

"I have completed my calculations," Blop said. He sounded annoyed. "It was a big project. A lot of work."

"Sorry, Blop. Tell us what you know," Leo said. He opened the tube and fished out an envelope and a maple bar donut.

"Gov, my man!" Remi said, snatching up the donut and ripping into it hungrily.

"The value of four pounds of A-plus-plus-plus Whippet estate diamonds is . . ." Blop had the answer on the tip of his robot tongue, but Leo had the envelope open and started talking excitedly before Blop could finish.

"Ten million dollars and change!" Leo yelled. "Yes!"

"Ten million, thirteen thousand, and twenty-one dollars, to be exact," Blop said. There was satisfaction in his voice, for he had been correct and this made him happy.

Leo continued reading the letter from the governor: "'Present enclosed certificate of payment to subcontractor: Ms. Lenora Sparks. Adult eyewitness must be present. Keep carbon copy. Complete transaction before midnight to avoid auction. I tried to reach you. For three years. I want that noted. Depositing extra funds in escrow. You're clear for at least a year. Enjoy the donut! The Gov.'"

Remi had munched down half the maple donut and handed the other half to Leo.

"How much time do we have?" Remi asked, wiping his sticky hands on Leo's overalls.

"I don't know for sure, maybe forty-five minutes. Possibly less." Leo stuffed the rest of the donut in his mouth all at once. He was a little bit of a stress eater when donuts and worry were in the same place at the same time.

"All we have to do is get back upstairs and we're home free!" Remi said. "How hard can that be?"

The trouble was, they still hadn't found hapless Mr. Carp.

"He only had one job, to keep an eye on us," Leo said, shaking his head. "And now *we* can't even find *him*."

Remi wasn't one to leave a man behind, even if he'd barely met him and he was the enemy.

"We can't just leave him down here. He'll never get out. Who'll take care of his cat?"

Leo looked around the cave at all the sparkling diamonds and thought of all they'd accomplished. They had the iron box, the zip rope, and the four Floogers. And they had paid the taxes on the hotel — Leo had a piece of paper to prove it. They decided to have Remi hold on to it, because of the flaps on his red doorman's jacket. The note would be safe in there.

But none of that changed the fact that Remi was right: They couldn't leave Mr. Carp behind.

"What are we going to do?" Leo wondered out loud.

And then the question answered itself.

It came in the form of a sound from outside the diamond mine: the clanging of a pipe and the sound of a man yelling "Ouch!"

Mr. Carp had stumbled within earshot, and with thirty-seven minutes to go, Remi and Leo bolted for the Realm of Gears as fast as their feet would carry them.

· CHAPTER 12 ·

MERGANZER'S PLAN UNFOLDS

It was Ms. Sparks who felt it first: a faraway trembling from somewhere under her feet.

The first tremors of an earthquake? she thought. But she knew better, and a split second later, another thought crossed her mind.

Merganzer is up to his old tricks again.

She tried to imagine what he could be doing that made the hotel tremble as it did. Was it some sort of strange magic? Were there a million ducks stampeding across the grounds, flown in to land in her hair and drive her away? She fussed and fretted in the quiet of the hotel lobby until she couldn't stand it any longer.

"I must have some air," she said, looking at her watch.

Thirty-five minutes! she thought as she walked.

Thirty-five little minutes and the Whippet Hotel would be hers! And then, very soon after, a wrecking ball would get rid of the Whippet for good. She could see it as she stood outside in the garden, gazing up at the hotel's puny silhouette against the great skyscrapers crowding in around it.

"You are a bad hotel," Ms. Sparks said. "A useless, ridiculous blight on the great state of New York!"

She felt something near her feet and thought it was Claudius, the cat. But when she looked down, she saw that nothing was there. The ground was trembling again, a little harder this time, and looking up once more at the Whippet Hotel, she could have sworn it was moving.

She ran up the front steps in search of Mr. Yancey, yelling, "You cannot stop me now, Merganzer D. Whippet! There's no time! You've lost! Lost, I tell you!"

She went on cackling, racing through the lobby only minutes before the auction.

She was right about one thing:

The Whippet Hotel *was* moving.

"Leo!" Remi cried. "The gears are moving!"

They'd come out of the tunnel into the huge expanse of the Realm of Gears. It was not as they had left it.

Like a beast the size of a cruise ship waking from a dream, the gears were groaning to life, shaking off dirt and rust, turning slowly and loudly.

"Mr. Carp!" Leo yelled, but he had fled out into the middle of the chaos.

"Mr. Carp, come back!" Remi tried. The gears were moving faster, causing other things to happen. Pulleys and enormous chains went up and down and round and round.

"Watch out!" Leo warned as a pendulum swung low through the space they were standing in. Leo shoved Remi out of the way just in time, and they crashed to the floor. Blop, who had been safely sitting in Remi's pocket, popped out and skidded across the floor, landing hard against a rolling gear. As the gear kept turning, Blop went with it, lodged between the metal teeth.

"What! No way!" Remi yelled, running toward his little friend. Leo gave chase, yelling Carp's name, hoping he would come to his senses.

"Hold on, Blop! I'm coming!" Remi said. Blop was not the kind of robot that could hold on to things, but he was good and wedged where he was either way. He didn't need to hold on.

Remi leapt onto the turning gear, holding on for dear life.

"Remi, be careful!" Leo called as the gear rolled Remi slowly up in the air. Remi climbed the wide iron teeth as it moved, reaching Blop at the same time the gear was about to turn both of them facedown toward the ground. It took some pulling and heaving, but Remi got Blop out in the nick of time, threw his pet robot into Leo's outstretched arms, and log-rolled onto the ground as the teeth of the gear disappeared under him.

There was no time for congratulations or high fives. Leo had seen the direction Mr. Carp had run in. He picked Remi up, and together they ran after him.

Over, under, and around gears.

"Mr. Carp, please!" Leo yelled, but it was so loud in the Realm of Gears that poor Mr. Carp couldn't hear them. He seemed to be going from gear to gear, searching for a way out, lost in his own attempt to find the exit.

"Hey, wait a minute," Remi said, grabbing his brother by the arm and stopping short.

"The envelope about the Realm of Gears — I have it!" Remi pulled his jacket open and took out the envelope they'd both forgotten about. The wax seal was still unbroken, the words black as coal on the manila envelope: *Open only when traveling in the Realm of Gears.*

"In all the chaos I totally forgot about that!" Leo said, slapping his head. "Open it! Quick!"

They kept on running as Remi broke the seal on the envelope. Whatever Merganzer D. Whippet had designed the Realm of Gears to do, it was doing one thing for sure: waking up. The gears, the pendulums, the riveted beams of steel — everything was moving faster and faster, like a speeding locomotive careening out of control.

"Mr. Carp! Where are you?!" Leo screamed, but it was no use. He thought he'd caught sight of him between the gears, way off in the distance, but it looked like he was running scared, searching for a place to hide, entirely unaware of Leo and Remi.

"Leo, wait," Remi said. The two boys stopped between a tower of enormous, turning clock parts rising into the air a hundred feet overhead.

Remi handed the paper to Leo, which only had a few words of instruction. It wasn't at all what Leo had expected. He'd thought there would be details and diagrams about how it had been built — and, more important, how to shut the crazy thing off!

Instead, he found two warnings:

WARNING:
WHEN THE GEARS MOVE,
YOU MUST MAKE THE PUZZLE QUICKLY!

"Leo, we have to leave. Now!" Remi shouted.

The Realm of Gears had gotten so loud and perilous, Leo could barely hear what Remi was saying. He couldn't stand leaving Mr. Carp behind, but what else could he do? Hopefully the puzzle would tell them what to do and they could come back and find him.

"Come on!" Leo said. "Let's make that puzzle!"

Remi and Leo dodged countless dangers as they zigged and zagged their way across the Realm of Gears. They found the door, burst through, and kept on running into the dark corridor, up the stairs, into the elevator shaft.

Completely out of breath, they dropped through the trapdoor and slid the rainbow card along the corner of the duck elevator. It was then that they realized, as the door slid open, that they had no more fuses. They'd forgotten to ask Dr. Flart for another, and there was no time to go back.

"This is a disaster!" Leo said. It was a rare and difficult feeling for a boy with great passion, a feeling of being defeated after trying so hard. He slumped down, tired and dejected, and felt the aches and pains of many bumps and bruises.

"It's okay, bro," Remi said, trying to comfort Leo. "Remember what Merganzer said?"

"Merganzer said a lot of things," Leo responded. He was looking at the puzzle key card, which he had pulled out of his maintenance overalls. "Unless you can climb like Loopa, I think we're stuck."

"Oh, but you're wrong," Remi said. He fished Blop out of his pocket and held him tight. "Sorry, little buddy. I'll put your head back on, promise."

Remi spun Blop's small head to one side, like he was taking the lid off a jar of peanut butter, and the head came off.

"I don't know why that bothers me so much," Remi said. "It's like he's really alive, you know? And I've just removed his brain."

Remi dug his fingers down inside the opening and popped a fuse out.

"Remi," Leo said, beaming, "what would I do without you? You're brilliant!"

Remi screwed Blop's head back on, but the robot didn't move. Its eyes wouldn't even open.

"It's okay, we can get another one, I'm sure of it," Leo said. He took the fuse and leaned through the opening, hanging his head below the duck elevator. A few seconds later, Leo had the old fuse out and the new one in.

"Here we go!" Remi said. He was excited as Leo

slipped back inside and the wall flew shut. Remi did the honors, pressing the lobby button as the elevator blasted up the shaft.

When they arrived at the lobby level, the doors came open and both boys crawled out. The hotel was rumbling oddly, in a way that Leo had never felt before. It scared him as they ran past the empty reception desk and into the Puzzle Room.

"Why is the hotel shaking?" Leo asked as they stared at the piles of puzzle pieces sliding onto the floor by the thousands.

"It must be the gears," Remi answered, looking at the very large duck-shaped clock on the wall across the room. "It's eleven fifty-two, Leo. We only have eight minutes left to pay Ms. Sparks!"

Leo didn't squander any more time wondering what had gone wrong with his hotel. He activated the puzzle key card and the screen lit up.

"Here goes," Leo said, not sure of what to expect. He'd seen the puzzle make itself before, but it had been a while and the magic had faded in his memory. Seeing it now — pieces flying everywhere in a storm of a million parts — took his breath away.

The puzzle began to snap together, which made a sound like an endless deck of cards being shuffled.

"Where is everyone?" Remi asked. "I bet Mr. Phipps

and Captain Rickenbacker wish they were here. They love this puzzle."

Leo had been wondering the same thing. The hotel felt oddly empty in a way he'd never felt before. And dark. Most of the lights were out; even the Puzzle Room was cast in a shadowy glow.

"I see the roof of the Whippet!" Leo said, the puzzle coming together fast now.

"What are those things on the corners of the roof?" Remi asked. "And that thing in the middle?"

Leo and Remi watched as the last thousand pieces dropped into place. Then they stood on two chairs at the table and looked down at the masterpiece. The other side of the puzzle had been a scene of the grounds and the ducks, but this was different.

This was a set of instructions.

"Those are the four Floogers!" Remi yelled.

"And the zip rope," Leo said, amazed at what they were both looking at.

The puzzle had pieced together a view of the top of the Whippet Hotel from the sky. In each corner of the roof there was a blue tube of light — four Floogers — and in the center, tied to a golden duck, an orange line disappearing into the sky — the zip rope.

Along the bottom of the huge puzzle, in Merganzer D. Whippet's script, were these words:

The Whippet moves! A rare surprise.
To the roof! Beware of spies!

"There you are!" Mr. Phipps said. He and Captain Rickenbacker had appeared at the door. "We were worried you might be trapped upstairs."

"What do you mean, *trapped*?" Remi asked.

"You don't know?" Mr. Phipps asked, astonished at how anyone could be left unaware of what was happening to the Whippet Hotel.

Captain Rickenbacker had taken a keen interest in the puzzle, standing on a chair of his own and looking down with his arms folded across his chest like he was Spider-Man gazing down at a city in trouble.

"The hotel has gone mad," Mr. Phipps said. "There's no other way to say it."

Leo didn't understand at all. He only knew that two important tasks lay before him: Pay Ms. Sparks and get to the roof.

"Where is Ms. Sparks hiding?" Leo asked. "We have what she wants. We can get rid of her, but we only have" — Leo looked at the duck-shaped clock on the wall — "two minutes!"

Leo pushed the appropriate buttons on the touch screen for the puzzle, and the entire thing burst into a million pieces, showering Captain Rickenbacker as he covered himself with his red cape.

"Better if no one else sees it," Leo said, running for the lobby as he asked Remi, "You remember what it showed us?"

"I do! I have a photo-puzzlic memory!"

Remi smiled despite the chaos all around him, but his smile faded into a look of dire concern as he dug into his red jacket pocket and found that the ten million dollar note from the governor of New York was missing. He stopped, fished around inside the pocket, looked inside, turned it inside out.

"What are you waiting for? Come on!" Leo said. "There's no time to waste!"

But Leo knew when he turned around and spotted the look on Remi's face. His brother's eyebrows were furled, his forehead was crinkled. Remi was nervous.

"What is it?" Leo asked, looking out the doors where he saw Ms. Sparks and Mr. Yancey standing alone on the grounds. They were a little ways off, looking up at the Whippet Hotel with looks of amazement on their faces.

"Leo," Remi said. Leo saw that his brother was on the verge of tears. "I lost it. I lost the money for Ms. Sparks, the money for the hotel."

Leo didn't know what to say. His fine hotel, the most wonderful hotel in the world, was in real trouble. It felt like it was about to crumble to the ground. *Something* was happening to it. And now this! Even in a pile of rubble, he couldn't imagine a Whippet Hotel owned by Mr. Yancey or Ms. Sparks. It was unthinkable.

"Come on," Leo said, turning for the front desk. "There's only one thing left for us to do. We have to get to the roof and do what the puzzle says. Maybe we can at least save the hotel from falling."

Leo quickly made a Double Helix card at the front desk and ushered Remi through a little orange door near the registration desk. Seconds later they were careening out of control, twisting and turning to the roof in the fastest contraption the Whippet had to offer.

"I'm sorry, Leo," Remi said. He felt terrible, as crummy as crummy gets.

It was hard to comfort someone while traveling through the Whippet at breakneck speed, but Leo tried. He put a hand on Remi's shoulder.

"It's going to be okay. We'll figure it out. We always do."

Remi brightened, then smiled, then howled at the amazing ride they were on.

"I love this hotellllllll," Remi screamed as they went. Both boys laughed despite all the bad news, enjoying the Whippet Hotel to the last, reveling in what it had come to mean to them both: adventure, friendship, and a belief that anything was possible if they let their imaginations run free.

They were out of the Double Helix in a flash when it arrived on the roof, and it was then that they finally understood something really strange was happening to the hotel. At first it felt like they'd gotten off a fair ride, which they sort of had, but it quickly became clear that the hotel was moving in a circle.

"Should we take a look over the edge, just for a moment?" Leo asked. He was overcome with curiosity and didn't have to wait for an answer. Remi was already running for one of the ledges, where some of the ducks were sitting, looking out at the spinning skyline.

When they leaned over the rail and got a good look at the rest of the hotel, they saw that each of the floors of the hotel was spinning. It was like there was a long pole up the middle of the Whippet, and each of the floors was spinning of its own free will.

"Best hotel *ever*!" Remi shouted.

The levels were spinning in different directions and at different speeds, and when Leo and Remi's side came around to where everyone was standing on the grounds, they waved and laughed.

"We better get to work," Leo said. "I'll do the zip rope, you put the four Floogers in place!"

"Done!" Remi said, and they both ran off in different directions. Leo kept wondering how and why in the world the Whippet was spinning as it was, but he knew the best chance of getting an answer would be to follow the instructions Merganzer had given him. The faster he could finish, the sooner he would know what Merganzer's grand plan was.

"Leo, it's working!" Remi yelled from a far corner of the roof. He'd found a small zigzag-shaped opening on a stone slab and dropped the Flooger inside. "It's making a weird humming sound, and it's gone!"

Gone, Leo thought. The Flooger had vanished into the Whippet Hotel, and it was humming. He wished that Dr. Flart was there to tell them what it meant. The Whippet's mad scientist would surely have known. Instead Leo stood in the very center of the roof watching the world spin around him. There he found the golden duck.

"And another!" Remi shouted. He was down to only two Floogers, and Leo hadn't even tied the zip rope to the golden duck. There was a reason for this, one that Remi, in his race to finish his task, hadn't noticed. Remi hadn't looked up, but Leo had an intuition about what was happening. He simply knew, before he turned his eyes up to the night sky, that Merganzer had arrived. A voice filled the air, and Remi finally stopped what he was doing and looked skyward.

"Hello, Leo! Hello, Remi! Such a lovely night, don't you think?"

Merganzer D. Whippet was leaning out the window of the blimp, waving at them with a smile on his face. The blimp, as before, seemed to blend in with the reflecting colors of night in Manhattan. All the lights and angles appeared to push right though the blimp, like the blimp was a ghost that only existed in Leo's and Remi's imaginations.

"I'm afraid we're running a tad behind schedule," Merganzer said. "We'll need to move fast."

A rope was thrown over and uncoiled until the end hung in front of Leo's face.

"Tie the zip rope to the golden duck and to the end of this rope, Leo. Quickly now. We really must be getting on with it."

Merganzer looked at Remi, who had already gone back to inserting Floogers and was down to the last.

"Got it!" Leo shouted, having tied the zip rope as tight as he could around the belly of the golden duck and attached the other end to the rope.

"Perfect!" Merganzer said, and he began to haul the rope up into the sky, arm over arm as the zip rope stretched. "It gets stronger, did Ingrid tell you that?"

"You mean the more it stretches?" Leo yelled up into the sky.

"Yes! But it reaches a point where it won't stretch any farther. That's when a zip rope is at its strongest."

"We got it from Loopa. She's a monkey," Remi yelled. He was finished with the Floogers and stood empty-handed next to Leo.

Merganzer had the end of the zip rope in his hand, having stretched it thirty feet into the air, and removed the regular rope.

"She is a good monkey, I can tell. This is a fine zip rope. The best."

Both boys beamed. They had bad news to share about the hotel, but Merganzer had a way of saying things that made them feel on top of the world, like everything was going to be okay after all.

"You might want to brace yourselves now," Merganzer said. "Could get a little bumpy."

Merganzer disappeared into the cab of the blimp.

"What do you think he's doing?" Remi asked.

"Something important, like pressing buttons and pushing levers. Come on, let's go to the edge. I have a feeling I know what's coming next."

Leo had been right. Merganzer D. Whippet *was* pressing buttons and pushing levers. The four Floogers began to glow hot and blue where they were trapped. Four thick bands of blue light appeared, one from each Flooger, rising over the roof and into the sky above.

They met at the bottom of the blimp, like four thick ropes of light that held the hotel level with their weird energy.

The blimp began to move up, up, and away as the zip rope stretched farther and farther. Leo was sure it was about to finally snap in two, but the zip rope held, stretching into the air.

The Whippet Hotel began to slow, and then it stopped spinning altogether.

"I see you up there, Leo Fillmore!" Ms. Sparks screamed up at the head poking over the edge of the roof. "Say good-bye to your hotel!"

She waved the letter from the governor that gave her the power to auction off the Whippet, laughing up at the two boys.

Leo had a moment of deep sorrow. He had lost the Whippet. He was sure of it. No matter what happened now, he would never walk the halls of the wackiest hotel in the world again as its owner. Ms. Sparks would ruin it — maybe even tear it down, a tragedy Leo could hardly bring himself to believe.

And then, just as all hope seemed lost, the Whippet Hotel began to move again. Only this time, it was the roof that moved and nothing else. The rest of the hotel had stopped, quiet and still, as if watching for something secret and rare about to take place.

"Leo," Remi said. "Did you feel that?"

"I did," Leo answered. "I think we're about to go for a ride."

The top floor of the Whippet Hotel, which included the roof and the library, lifted free.

"A very good monkey!" Merganzer yelled out the window. "It's holding beautifully!"

The blimp began to rise faster, like it had finally pulled itself free from stakes tied to the ground, and the top floor of the Whippet rose with it.

Five feet, then ten, then fifty feet into the air. It wobbled softly, but there was magic or science or both at work on the roof of the Whippet Hotel that night, and it stayed almost completely level.

"There must be something about the Floogers that keeps it steady," Remi said, laughing. He couldn't *stop* laughing. It was just so perfect; a breathtaking event he had helped set in motion. Unimaginable, and yet it was happening!

"Here he comes!" Leo shouted, pointing up into the sky where the buildings were flying past as the blimp rose higher still. Merganzer D. Whippet was sliding down the zip rope like it was a fire engine pole. He slowed on his final approach, then touched down in his long jacket and perfectly shined shoes.

"Don't try that without gloves." He smiled. "A zip rope will give you the king of all rug burns."

Remi was laughing, smiling, hopping up and down with enthusiasm. But Leo couldn't join in the excitement. He stared at the ground on the verge of tears. He simply couldn't bring himself to tell Merganzer he'd failed to pay the taxes. The Whippet Hotel was lost, or at least most of it.

Merganzer winked at Remi, then knelt down next to Leo and touched the underside of his chin, lifting Leo's head. He looked into Leo's eyes.

"Dear boy, don't cry."

And that did it. Leo did cry, just one tear that rolled down his cheek. Merganzer flicked the tear away with his gloved finger and smiled.

"But you don't understand," Leo said. "I lost the hotel. It's gone."

"You see there," Merganzer said, glancing at Remi. "I always knew I picked the right man for the job."

"I don't understand." Leo sniffed, frustrated that Merganzer wouldn't listen. "I lost the hotel. Ms. Sparks owns it now. Don't you see?"

"No, that's not true. You only think it's true."

Leo felt butterflies in his chest.

Could it be?

Was it possible Merganzer had a plan Leo didn't know about?

Merganzer D. Whippet looked at his watch, then pulled a key card out of his jacket pocket. Only it wasn't a key card.

"All is well, I assume?" Merganzer said, talking into the card like it was a phone.

"All is well," came a voice Leo and Remi knew. "And you? Dr. Flart and Ingrid will want to know — how are the Floogers and the zip rope working?"

"Very well, thank you. Please give them my best. And thank you, Karl, you've done well."

"Anytime, sir. Anytime at all."

"Better finish things up, the clock has struck twelve," Merganzer said.

He put the key card back in his jacket and stood, staring down at the two boys.

They were speechless, and as Merganzer clapped his hands twice, the rope ladder unfurled out of the blimp.

"I can see you're confused, as I suspected you might be," Merganzer said. "Let's get aboard the blimp, then I'll tell you everything. Right-o?"

"Who's driving?" Remi asked.

"George, of course," Merganzer said. George Powell, his oldest and dearest friend, waved down from above as Merganzer went on. "It's very good to have a wing-man, don't you think?"

Remi nodded, putting his arm around Leo. "It's the best."

Bewildered by the wonder of it all, Leo and Remi started climbing while things took shape on the ground below.

———

Ms. Sparks and Mr. Yancey, overcome with the sight of what was happening to the Whippet Hotel, had let the clock tick past midnight without completing their trans-action. They'd marveled as the levels turned around and around, wondering what it could possibly mean. Then they'd seen the top of the Whippet Hotel rise into the air, carried away in the night sky.

An argument between two greedy people had then broken out.

"It's worth a little less now, don't you think?" Mr. Yancey had asked. "I mean, with the missing floor and all. What will we do if it rains? There's no roof. And there must be some structural damage after all that . . . *spinning.*"

"Taxes are taxes, you buffoon," Ms. Sparks had said. "We were going to rip it down anyway. Now it will be easier."

"Still, it is one less floor," Mr. Yancey persisted. He was a slave to his real estate sensibilities. "Has to count for something, one would think."

"Are you deliberately ignoring me?" Ms. Sparks asked. "We're going to knock it over anyway! Now we'll have less rubble to deal with. It's a bonus."

Mr. Yancey had begun to dial his phone in search of his lawyer when Jane Yancey came running over with Loopa, the monkey. She'd placed the monkey in a toy stroller and dressed her in doll clothes.

"Daddy! This pet is sick. All it wants to do is sleep."

Loopa had eaten twelve cupcakes, given to her by Jane Yancey, so she did have a stomachache.

"I'm busy right now, Jane. This will have to wait."

"But it won't wait! This is important!"

While Jane Yancey threw a fit, the long-stay guests — Captain Rickenbacker, LillyAnn Pompadore, and Theodore Bump — moved a little closer. So did Nancy Yancey and Mr. Phipps, who had been listening but acting as though they were not. They'd all come streaming out of the hotel as they figured out it was spinning in circles, and the gathering crowd did not suit Ms. Sparks one bit.

"Mr. Yancey!" she shouted. "Let us complete our transaction, shall we?"

Mr. Yancey, sensing the opportunity slipping from his hands, looked at his wife. She nodded — *Get on with it!* — and he took a sealed envelope from the jacket of his three-thousand-dollar suit.

Jane Yancey was stomping around her toy stroller yelling, "Sick monkey! Sick monkey!" over and over again with her arms crossed over her chest and a scowl on her face.

"It's a floor short of a hotel, but all right. My sealed bid is in the envelope," Mr. Yancey said.

Ms. Sparks was beaming. She lifted her long fingers out toward the prize, thinking of a wrecking ball swinging through the air toward the Whippet Hotel.

"That won't be necessary," someone said. As fast as lightning — or so it seemed — a receipt was placed in Ms. Sparks's outstretched hand.

"Mr. Carp?" Ms. Sparks said. He was flanked on one side by Dr. Flart and the other by Ingrid. Dr. Flart hadn't been out of the dungeon in years. He was pale as a ghost and wearing his mad scientist white jacket. Ingrid's eyes zeroed in on Jane Yancey, who had gone suddenly quiet. And Mr. Carp, who had given Ms. Sparks the receipt, was covered in grease from his thick mustache all the way down to his grimy shoes, like he'd been fixing gears for hours, which in fact he had been.

"Give me back my monkey," Ingrid said. She was shorter than Jane Yancey, but no one stood between Ingrid and one of her animals. Jane was too terrified to speak and backpedaled into her mother's arms. When Ingrid had Loopa in her arms, she smiled down at her, then turned on Jane Yancey.

"Never dress a monkey. Or give it treats. Understood?"

Jane nodded fast, leaning into her mother, who was mortified.

"See," Mr. Bump mumbled to LillyAnn Pompadore. "I told you there was a monkey in the hotel."

"Not anymore there's not."

Ingrid had gotten what she came for and turned on a dime, marching back in the direction of the lobby.

"Dr. Flart," she said over her shoulder. "Will I be seeing you soon?"

There was a certain something in her voice that made Dr. Flart blush.

"I believe my duties are about to change," he said. "You'll be seeing me again."

Mr. Carp leaned down low and whispered into Captain Rickenbacker's ear. "Lovebirds, though they are very slow about their business. They've been close to holding hands for going on seven years."

"Remarkable," Captain Rickenbacker said.

"What is the meaning of this?!" Ms. Sparks yelled. She could feel the wheels coming off of her plan but didn't know what to do. It was all so confusing!

"Ms. Sparks," Mr. Carp said. "You hold in your hand a copy of a receipt showing full payment of taxes to the great state of New York. The Whippet Hotel is, in fact, more than a year ahead on its payments as of earlier this evening. I'm afraid the auction will not be taking place."

"But that's impossible! We had a deal, you little sea urchin!"

Dr. Flart was the one person in the group tall enough to look down at Ms. Sparks. He even towered over her tall beehive hairdo. He stepped between Mr. Carp and Ms. Sparks and leaned down, staring at her through his thick glasses.

"Why is this hideous man staring at me?" Ms. Sparks asked, but no one answered her.

Claudius purred against Ms. Sparks's leg, startling her.

"Hello, cat!" Dr. Flart said, picking up Claudius and petting him with great enthusiasm. Claudius tried to squirm free, but it was no use. "I've been looking everywhere for you!"

"Sorry about that," Mr. Carp said. "You were out and I needed a little something to sell the idea."

"Have I got an experiment for you!" Dr. Flart said, which made Claudius go wide-eyed with concern. Dr. Flart wandered off toward the lobby, happy to have his cat and return to his very important work. Over his shoulder he said, "Breakfast tomorrow, Karl? I have something new to show you."

"I thought you might," Mr. Carp answered. "Wouldn't miss it."

Ms. Sparks was starting to back away toward the gate, for she knew that she was once again defeated. She couldn't quite understand how or why, but she was sure her plans had failed her when she heard, from way up high in the sky, the wild and whimsical laugh of Merganzer D. Whippet.

"This is not over!" she said, turning for the gate. "Not even close! I will prevail!"

"She's fun to have around," Captain Rickenbacker said. "Never a dull moment."

"So true, so true," said Mr. Phipps. "Shall we work on the puzzle and have a root beer?"

"And then some pinball!"

"Might I join you?" Ms. Pompadore asked.

"Me, too," Theodore Bump piped in. "I don't feel like writing a novel tonight. There's magic in the air."

And with that, Captain Rickenbacker and Mr. Phipps and the others were moving off. Mr. Yancey was on the phone, calling a limo to take his family away, ignoring Jane complaining about her missing monkey. They, too, moved off together in search of an expensive restaurant to make themselves feel better.

Mr. Carp stood alone on the grounds of the Whippet Hotel, staring up at the sky, where a blimp was moving quietly and secretly to places unknown to him. He took a key card out of his pocket with his greasy hand and talked into it.

"All finished up here," he said. "Taxes paid, hotel at rest, gears stopped once again."

"You have done very, very well," Merganzer answered. "You are, without a doubt, a man of many talents."

"Thank you, sir. It was a little touch-and-go at the end. Tell Remi I found the note from the governor where he dropped it. It's all taken care of."

Mr. Carp could hear Remi whooping and hollering in the background.

"Can I return to my work?" Mr. Carp asked. "Some problems down there."

"Of course," Merganzer said. "And keep an eagle eye on things in the hotel for another week, won't you? I have need of Leo and Remi. Big things. Big things!"

Mr. Carp smiled and said he would. He looked once more into the night sky, waved, and began walking toward his true home.

"Oh yes, he's brilliant," Merganzer said. They were far above the city, moving silently below the clouds. "One of my best men."

"So Mr. Carp works for you?" Remi asked. He was still terribly confused, trying to piece it all together.

"They all do, but Mr. Carp is my favorite. You might say he's my underground wingman."

Mr. Powell, at the wheel of the blimp, winked at Leo. "Merganzer is the only fellow I know who needs two wingmen, one below and one above ground."

"I am terribly forgetful about taxes and bills. I have no idea why," Merganzer said. "It's the strangest thing. Anywho, Ms. Sparks was aware of my shortcomings. She knew I'd forget, knew how to manipulate the system. By the time George reminded me for the ninth time, it was too late. Too dangerous. I needed to bring in Mr. Carp."

"He seems so . . . I don't know." Leo tried to find the words. "Harmless, I guess."

Mr. Powell laughed, turning the blimp to the right as he did.

"You won't believe it's true, but he built the Realm of Gears," Merganzer said.

"And most of the hotel, too," Mr. Powell added.

"Did not," Remi said. He simply couldn't believe

someone as drab and boring as Mr. Carp could be so smart and resourceful.

"Oh, but he did," Merganzer said. "And he's quite good at playing the part of a tax agent as well."

"The role was tailor-made for Mr. Karl Carp," Mr. Powell said. "He was perfect."

Betty flew up from the roof and landed on the ledge of the cab, honking.

"I do love a good duck," Merganzer said, fishing around in his pocket for a treat. "It will be good to have them with me again."

"Why in the world did you pull the top of your hotel off?" Remi asked. Remi was a great question asker, everyone agreed.

"Well, I wanted the ducks with me, so there's that," Merganzer said. "But it's so much more. You see, I'm working on something big. The biggest."

"Huge," Mr. Powell said.

"And I knew the day would come when I'd need my books, my plans, my notes."

"You mean your library?" Leo asked, for really, that's what they were carrying across the sky.

"Precisely! The library. But not just the library; something else, too."

"What?" Leo asked.

"Why, I needed you, of course," he said, putting one arm around Remi and one around Leo.

Leo and Remi smiled and looked at each other. For whatever reason, they had been handpicked by Merganzer D. Whippet to own the hotel, travel through its many rooms and secret places, and fly across the sky in the middle of the night.

"Oh!" Leo said, remembering that he had one more item for Merganzer, something he'd asked for. Leo fished the iron box out of his maintenance overalls and held it out.

"Is the Wyro inside?" Merganzer asked, awed and delighted.

"See for yourself," Leo said, tossing it into the air and watching Merganzer catch it.

"Light as a feather," Merganzer marveled. "And safely strapped inside with duct tape. I wish I'd invented that one."

"So does Dr. Flart," Remi said.

"Well," Merganzer said, smiling with deep satisfaction, "this calls for a toast."

Merganzer tossed the iron box to Mr. Powell, who regarded it as something extremely dangerous and volatile. He gently placed it in a basket under the steering wheel and sighed with relief.

Leo was happy the hotel was still his and, more importantly, that it was safe. He was excited about the adventure under the hotel he and Remi were a part of. He was glad Ms. Sparks, at least for one night, was not a threat.

But he'd been wanting to ask about something else, and finally he did.

"Where are we going, Merganzer D. Whippet?"

Merganzer gazed out over the city below, which shimmered with lights. He knelt down and turned away from Leo and Remi, opening a small refrigerator. When he turned back around, he held four bottles of Flart's Fizz in his hands.

"Flart's Fizz!" Remi said. "Oh man, I hope I don't get a dud!"

Merganzer handed out the bottles and they all popped the tops at the same time.

"My last four bottles," Merganzer said. And then he made the toast: "To the field of wacky inventions, where anything is possible!"

They all agreed at once. "To the field of wacky inventions!"

And then they drank and burped and laughed.

Leo would soon find that by *anything*, Merganzer really did mean *anything*.

Some of those things were scary (like the genetically altered twelve-foot chicken).

Some were dangerous (the electric eel ponds, for one, were a terrible hazard).

And some Merganzer had lost complete control of (things that went bump in the night had become especially difficult to manage).

Troubles were mounting far below, waiting to be had.

But on that one night, burping like sailors as they moved unseen across the city, all was well in the world of Leo, Remi, and Merganzer D. Whippet.

Made in United States
Troutdale, OR
11/14/2024

24426374R00136